...As soon as he laid her naked on the bed, pulling off his own clothes and joining her, she began to change—into a fierce young animal that wanted to smother death and loss with the fire and oblivion of passion...

Other books by
J. D. HARDIN

BLOOD, SWEAT AND GOLD
THE GOOD, THE BAD, AND THE DEADLY
THE SLICK AND THE DEAD
BULLETS, BUZZARDS, BOXES OF PINE
FACE DOWN IN A COFFIN
THE MAN WHO BIT SNAKES
THE SPIRIT AND THE FLESH
BLOODY SANDS
RAIDER'S HELL
RAIDER'S REVENGE
HARD CHAINS, SOFT WOMEN
RAIDER'S GOLD
SILVER TOMBSTONES
DEATH LODE
COLDHEARTED LADY
GUNFIRE AT SPANISH ROCK
SONS AND SINNERS
DEATH FLOTILLA
SNAKE RIVER RESCUE
THE LONE STAR MASSACRE
BOBBIES, BAUBLES AND BLOOD
BIBLES, BULLETS AND BRIDES
HELLFIRE HIDEAWAY
APACHE GOLD
SASKATCHEWAN RISING
HANGMAN'S NOOSE
BLOODY TIME IN BLACKTOWER
THE MAN WITH NO FACE
THE FIREBRANDS
DOWNRIVER TO HELL
BOUNTY HUNTER
QUEENS OVER DEUCES
CARNIVAL OF DEATH
SATAN'S BARGAIN
THE WYOMING SPECIAL
LEAD-LINED COFFINS

J.D. HARDIN

SAN JUAN
SHOOTOUT

BERKLEY BOOKS, NEW YORK

SAN JUAN SHOOTOUT

A Berkley Book/published by arrangement with
the author

PRINTING HISTORY
Berkley edition/June 1984

ISBN: 0-425-07257-6

CHAPTER ONE

A stagecoach still operated twice a week through Lagrange down into Cheyenne, where passengers could board the railroad running east and west, from coast to coast, one of the true wonders of modern civilization. A branch line of the railroad ran from Cheyenne to Denver and south. But up in the prairies drained by the Horse and Lodgepole creeks, a man rode his own horse or he caught the stage.

Eight passengers rode inside the coach, four facing forward and four to the rear, rubbing shoulders as the vehicle bounced and swayed in the deep ruts of the trail across the flat land. One man and his wife, both of them thin, quiet, and plainly dressed, kept their eyes to themselves, spoke to no one. It was easy to figure they were members of one of those old-style religions, out in the sinful world to buy some essentials. They seemed afraid the evil ways of strangers would rub off on them and stick.

Three men, cattle buyers for big stockyards back east, joked with one another about past business coups and cared little for their rivalry now that they were heading back to the comforts and pleasures of a big town. They wore business suits, and heavy gold watch chains looped across their generous paunches. Laughing loudly, they stroked their mustaches in anticipation of what lay ahead for them tonight in Cheyenne.

The three stockyard agents were scrupulous in their language, because of the presence of a pretty girl, perhaps eighteen at the most, and her mother, who looked a formidable basilisk. The men knew them as the wife and daughter of a well-to-do rancher, and the women told them they were on a shopping expedition to Cheyenne. The men remembered how they had heard some of the ranchers cussing about how their women wanted to go to San Francisco and even New York to shop now that the railroad made it possible—women who had been happy all their lives with a couple of trips to Cheyenne a year and maybe one to Denver. Now they were demanding to go halfway across the world to buy their fripperies and finery. Damn! It just went to show how vanity could put to misuse man's finest achievement—a transcontinental railroad!

No one said anything to the eighth man aboard the stage, and they waited till he lay snoring, half slipping off the seat, before they discussed him.

"I think the brute is drunk," the beautiful girl's mother said primly.

Her daughter tittered and glanced at the sleeping man with interest, until she received a sharp maternal elbow in the ribs.

"I dunno where he managed to find whiskey in this country," one of the cattle buyers said with envy. He gestured out the window at the tall waving grass that disappeared over every horizon in heaving swells.

Another wrinkled his nose appreciatively. "It's whiskey all right. No doubt about that. He went to sleep like a baby."

The third stockyard agent said, "I bet he's listening to every word we're saying right now. His kind don't sleep. They don't dare to."

That shut them all up for a while. They had noticed how the sleeping man's six-gun was cleaned and oiled, riding easy in its holster. The man had obviously lavished much more care on this weapon than on his own personal appearance. That meant only one thing to them. He was a gunfighter.

He had climbed aboard the coach earlier—a huge man, six foot two, with wide shoulders, skin tanned like leather, black drooping mustache, and jet black eyes. He had thrown his black Stetson on the rack over his head, along with his Winchester carbine. His sun-bleached denims and scarred leather jacket told of days and nights spent under the open sky. His feet, in battered calfskin Middleton boots, were stretched across the coach, forcing the passengers on the opposite seat to make room for them, as they listened to the stranger snore his way to Cheyenne.

Raider was catching his first decent sleep in three days. He had been in the saddle from sunup to sundown for the past two weeks, hunting three cattle thieves, sometimes with the sheriff and his deputies. The thieves had been running cattle down to the railroad and shipping them east. So the rail company was sensitive to charges that it was encouraging rustling in the area and hired a Pinkerton—Raider—to ride with the sheriff to make sure something was done. Raider had been the only one to do very much. And although he had not caught the three thieves, he had put a stop to their thieving. He guessed they had moved on to more rewarding country and made a three-day sweep of the rangeland, combined with all-night watches, to persuade himself the varmints had not just gone to ground, waiting for him to leave.

Raider hated to quit without having something in hand to show for his efforts. But there was no bonanza in scouring empty prairie for people who were no longer there. He was real sure the three thieves were gone.

As a Pinkerton, Raider could accept no money on the side from the agency's clients, but he sure as hell didn't turn down the bottle of whiskey offered him by a grateful rancher. It helped him pass the time while he waited for the stage into Cheyenne.

Raider snored on, unaware and anyway uncaring of the other passengers' reactions to him. The jolting of the coach gradually eased him off the bench seat, and when the wheels on one side dipped in a hollow, his body fell to the floor. He slept on.

"I've never seen anything quite so disgraceful," the girl's mother observed, drawing in her feet so they would not be touched by the sleeping man's sprawling body. "I can't understand why one of you gentlemen don't throw him off this coach."

None of the gentlemen present looked particularly comfortable about this idea.

"Let him be," one of them said. "He's harming no one."

The lady sniffed and pointedly ignored them from then on.

All of them, except for the severe thin man and his severe thin wife, had dozed off in the heat of the afternoon when the coach eased to a stop. They woke, one by one, aroused by the absence of the coach's jolting and rocking. They looked out the windows: The empty prairie stretched away boundlessly in every direction.

Three horsemen with leveled, double-barreled shotguns stood about the coach, one covering the driver and one on each side of the coach.

"Git out!" one of the horsemen yelled.

He had a growth of beard on his face, and his clothes were worn and sweat-stained. He definitely was the kind who meant what he said when he looked at people over the rims of two twelve-gauge barrels. The passengers hurried themselves out so he would not grow impatient at them. The horseman whistled in surprise when he saw the beautiful girl step down from the coach.

"We're going to take you along with us to see some of the sights." The outlaw grinned toothlessly at the girl and motioned to her with his shotgun. "Move over there, away from the others."

The mother clutched her terrified daughter and glared in defiance at the horseman.

He dismounted, pulled the daughter out of her grasp, and threw her on the ground some distance from her mother, whom he held at bay with the shotgun.

Meanwhile the other two horsemen were disarming and robbing the passengers, who stood in a line throwing their valuables at their feet.

In a moment of silence, they all distinctly heard a loud snore from inside the coach.

The gunman who had thrown the girl to the ground walked toward the coach and swung open its door. Instead of finding a sleeping man, he found himself looking into Raider's smiling face and the business end of his Remington .44.

"I see you changed your profession from rustling to holding up stages," Raider drawled as he squeezed the trigger. "Explains why I couldn't find you."

The heavy slug entered the open mouth of the bewildered bandit and blew out the back of his skull, scattering the gray pulp of his brain onto the green prairie grass.

Raider's next shot through the open door of the coach hit one of the horsemen high in the chest. The man's mouth opened as if he were about to say something, and a stream of blood issued from between his lips and ran down over his chin and onto his shirt. His eyes became very round and he toppled sideways from his saddle.

The third bandit had brought the barrels of his shotgun to bear on Raider and was about to squeeze the trigger when a .44 slug ripped away his left collarbone, snapping it like a chicken's wishbone, and a second lead projectile from the Remington six-gun plunged into his right eye—popping the eyeball in an instant and piercing the bone of the skull in the eye orbit to become lodged in the right cerebral hemisphere of the brain. The finger curled over the trigger of the shotgun never got the message to pull.

Raider climbed down from the coach, holstered his smoking revolver, stretched, and yawned.

He said to his fellow passengers in a puzzled voice, "Funny how you can spend two weeks looking for folks, and just after you've given up ever finding them, they show up unexpected and of their own accord."

Allan Pinkerton sat behind a large walnut desk in his office. "I have one very experienced operative due in Cheyenne this evening. I could send him."

"Better send two," the tight-lipped man with a bald head and gold pince-nez said.

The big man behind the desk frowned in disapproval at such extravagance. He said in a strong Scottish burr, "It'll cost ye good money."

"Mr. Pinkerton, money is the one thing our consortium of investors in New York have in abundance. What we lack are good ideas to make our money breed, grow, multiply."

"I see."

"I'm not sure you do," the man with the pince-nez continued. "We are not merely asking you to locate a missing man. Arcady T. Harrison is not merely a missing man, he is something much more important to us—a missing investment. Harrison's ideas are our assets. We bought them. Now we own them. Anyone who harms Harrison is damaging our property. Valuable property. We are prepared to pay for your two best men, and of course we'll cover all expenses involved."

"I keep a close watch over expenses," Pinkerton said enthusiastically.

The bald man pursed his narrow lips. "You have an

excellent reputation in the business world, Mr. Pinkerton."

"Thank you, sir."

"Let me acquaint you thoroughly with the situation, Mr. Pinkerton. Our investors were most impressed with some of the concepts developed by Arcady T. Harrison, especially those relating to the smelting of silver ore. You will understand when I say I am limited in what I am permitted to tell you of these processes, but suffice it to say that..."

The big Scotsman snorted impatiently as he listened to the man's loquacious and roundabout account of how a group of Wall Street financiers had sent an oddball inventor out to the San Juan silver fields in southwestern Colorado. The inventor's goal was to come up with a new smelting process that could be used at the mines, so that unpurified silver ore did not have to be carried hundreds of miles by burro over the mountains. The inventor made several reports to his employers in New York from a mining town named Mineral Point, and then disappeared without a trace.

Allan Pinkerton had heard a thousand stories like this before. For three reasons he had learned to restrain his natural pessimism about the chances of finding such a missing person alive. First, pessimism on his part was bad for business; second, people didn't want to hear what he had to say unless it agreed with their way of thinking; and third, his own operatives constantly surprised him with what they could accomplish. In the case of a few like Raider, they constantly amazed him with the trouble they could brew.

Pinkerton sat behind his big walnut desk in the headquarters of the Pinkerton National Detective Agency at 191–193 Fifth Avenue in Chicago, and he nodded his great head politely as the representative of the New York investors enlarged upon the financial threat involved in the disappearance of such a valuable asset as Arcady T. Harrison.

Pinkerton had come up the hard way himself and had little personal sympathy for a bunch of robber barons who had lost their performing monkey. His immigrant ship from Glasgow had sunk off Nova Scotia, and he and his wife had arrived in the New World by way of a lifeboat, without a single possession other than what they wore on their backs. But in spite of himself, Allan Pinkerton understood all too well what the investor was talking about, for he also depended wholly on the talent of others to achieve his success. He trained his men, bullied them, underpaid them, supported them in trouble—but ultimately depended upon only a few special operatives of particular talent to get the really tricky jobs done and uphold the reputation of the agency. Which was the only reason why he put up with Raider. Raider would almost certainly destroy part of this mining town of Mineral Point and kill a percentage of its inhabitants, but if this oddball inventor was to be found alive, Raider was the man to find him and bring him back in one piece.

"You mentioned that this Mr. Harrison, the lost inventor, is perhaps a little . . . eccentric at times?"

"Indeed yes, Mr. Pinkerton. One of the unfortunate man's blemishes of character is an unseemly appetite—one might even say a lust—for the fair sex. Apparently he continually throws over the development of an important project in order to pursue the charms of some less-than-virtuous woman. Those are the only kind he pursues, I've been told. Unfortunately, we knew nothing of this side of his personality until it was too late."

"Don't you think it possible he has just taken off for a short period on a romantic escapade?" Pinkerton inquired.

"This man is under contract to us," the investor replied stiffly. "There is no clause in our agreement which grants him leave for such irresponsible activities. He must be located and retrieved at once."

Pinkerton sighed. "We'll find him for you, sir, but we

can't bring him back against his will."

Pinkerton had already made up his mind who the second operative on the case would be—Doc Weatherbee, Raider's frequent partner and a good man to spread oil on the waters that Raider troubled.

"Doc Weatherbee!" the man pleaded, standing on a wooden kitchen chair in the middle of a stable.

"You got a fair offer," Doc told him. "Take it or leave it."

The man's hands were bound behind him, a noose was tightened about his neck, and the rope was knotted around a roof beam above his head.

"You're a Pinkerton," the man whined. "It ain't allowed for you to do this."

"It's not me who's doing anything," Doc replied suavely, gesturing at the silent, glowering men around them. "It's these fine folk here who want vengeance because you cheated them out of their money. I can't prove you did it and so can't arrest you. If you were in my custody, I could protect you."

"I'm guilty! Guilty!" the man shouted. "Arrest me!"

Doc shrugged. "I can't. I have no proof."

"I'll give you proof!"

"You will?"

"Don't hang me! Please God, don't hang me!"

Doc brushed an invisible speck of dust off his pearl-gray derby. "You mentioned some proof?"

The man stared at him sullenly. "I've confessed in front of all these witnesses. Ain't that enough?"

One of the ranchers yelled back an answer: "No, it ain't enough. You got our money hid somewheres, and you reckon you'll spend a little time in jail and come back and fetch it. You ain't never going to spend my money as a living man while I breathe air in Kansas."

The man on the chair gazed at Doc in mute appeal. Doc avoided his eyes.

Doc Weatherbee's appearance was in marked contrast to that of the rest of the men in the stable. They wore the usual ranch denims, shirts of sturdy cloth, well-worn boots, and battered broad-brimmed hats. Doc's gray derby had a curled-up brim, his shirt was silk, as was the pale blue vest that covered it, his suit was of the finest worsted wool, and his Melton overgaiters had five buttons. He was handsome, spoke with an educated eastern accent, and did not sprinkle his speech with cuss words. He carefully tended his big-city image out here in the rough rangelands of Kansas. Apart from the man with the noose around his neck, Doc was the only one in the stable not carrying a gun on his belt.

"If that money you claim to have stolen from the widow Brown were to show up," Doc said, "I'd have to take you in to stand trial. I wouldn't let any man here stop me from doing that."

The man standing on the chair said nothing.

The local ranchers had pooled their money, in the care of the widow Brown, whose stable this was, to buy out her breeding stock when she sold her land in the near future. Five thousand dollars in ten- and twenty-dollar gold pieces were stashed in two canvas sacks beneath the floorboards of her kitchen. The man with the rope around his neck had persuaded her to let him deposit the money in the town bank. He should have kept going at that point, but he came back for more—money and the widow. It so happened that the bank manager paid the widow Brown a social call with his wife the next day and knew nothing of any deposit. The bank manager told the widow to hold her peace. When he could not interest the sheriff, he telegraphed the Pinkerton National Detective Agency in Chicago. It so happened Weatherbee was nearby.

"Well, gentlemen," Doc said to the others, "I think there's nothing more for me to do here. I'll join Mrs. Brown for a cup of tea."

He made for the door, and the man with the noose around his neck called after him in a hoarse whisper, "Wait!"

"What for?" Doc asked impatiently.

"We gotta deal if I give back the money? You'll take me in alive?"

"You've got my word on that," Doc said.

"The gold is under a flat stone forty paces north of the henhouse. Just lift up the stone—the bags are right under it. The money's all there, 'cept for about forty dollars."

Five of the ranchers rushed out the door.

"I think I'll have that cup of tea while we wait," Doc said and exited after them.

When he returned ten minutes later, he had the widow Brown on his arm. She was petite, in her early thirties, and had long black hair and lonely, yearning, big brown eyes in a pretty face.

The man still stood on the chair with the rope around his neck. On the stable floor, the canvas sacks lay spilled of gold coins.

"There's more than forty dollars short," one rancher growled.

The widow looked shocked at the sight of the man in the noose. "Doc, I never thought you'd have a part in something like this"—she gave the man a look of contempt—"even for a sidewinder like this."

Doc walked forward to where the man stood on the wooden chair. "The money's more than forty dollars short. You deserve to hang."

"No!" the woman and condemned man gasped together.

Doc ignored them and kicked the chair out from beneath the man's legs, so that his body fell as a deadweight on the length of rope.

The rope snapped.

The man lay writhing on the ground in fear.

Then the truth dawned on him. "You bastard!" he snarled at Doc. "You tricked me. You cut the rope nearly all the way through before you put it around my neck."

"Of course," Doc agreed. "As you observed earlier, my friend, a Pinkerton would never permit a suspect to be strung up." He turned to the others. "I'll take him into town later. If you boys would allow me to have a word in private with the widow . . ."

He escorted her past the corral to the ranch house.

"I suppose you'll be moving on now," she said to him as they walked.

"I reckon so."

"I'm almost sorry you made him confess so soon," she said. "Pity you didn't delay it a while and stay around longer." She pinched him in the side playfully and let her fingers slide across his muscular belly. "You see what you're doing to me? Making me lose my widow's respectability."

"Hang onto it for another twenty-five yards," Doc said. "Then we'll be inside the house, and we can let ourselves go."

He slammed the door after them and caught her small strong body in his arms as she threw herself passionately upon him.

"I don't want you to leave," she sobbed. "Stay with me here and I won't sell the ranch."

Doc soothed her with a joke. "I'm not a cattleman—that kind of work would ruin my suit."

He pressed his mouth upon hers before she could answer, and his hands ran caressingly over the curves of her body. She responded willingly to his tactile suggestions. He felt her small breasts swell in his palms beneath the silky material of her dress, and her tongue met his in a titillating exchange.

Doc peeled her clothes away from her inviting flesh until she lay naked and quivering on a buffalo skin on the floor. He swiftly climbed out of his own clothes and joined her on the thick hide. His large hands stroked her petite torso, and the smooth feel of her skin inflamed his senses.

Running his lips and tongue over her entire body, he drove her into a frenzy of desire, so that she twisted and turned in hot lust under his masterful and tender touches. When she could stand it no more and called out desperately for him to enter her and ease her hunger, he lay between her legs and positioned the bulbous head of his member between the slippery lips of her sex. He slowly entered her and heard her moan with pleasure.

Her cunt was small and tight as her body, and gripped his member even more tightly than did her arms about his body. He felt the waves of sensation sweeping through her flesh, and the damp membranes of her sex throbbed and squeezed around his cock.

He drove up hard and fast and deep inside her, in swelling energy and surging excitement—and for one crazy moment swore to himself silently that he would never leave her, that he would quit the Pinkertons and stay here to fuck her on the buffalo skin forevermore.

CHAPTER TWO

The miner ran a work-hardened hand over his grizzled chin and squinted warily at the big gunman standing next to him at the bar. No matter what this fella claimed to be, the miner doubted he would ever see him with a pick and shovel working on the side of the mountain.

"Stand on the summit of Red Mountain," the miner said, "and look out all around you in every direction for a distance of fifteen miles, so that you are at the center of a circle thirty miles across. That circle, with Red Mountain at its center, is the most richly mineralized spot man has found on the face of the globe. It's what we call the San Juan."

Raider poured the miner a generous measure from his whiskey bottle and refilled his own glass. "Would it take a lot of skill for me to get started?"

The miner was not fooled. "It might take a lot of hard work."

Raider laughed. "Suppose I was willing to lather up a sweat, how would I go about finding ore?"

"King Solomon, Engineer Peak, and Mount Sneffles is just chockful of silver. The first ones of us out here just had to dig anywheres on any side of a mountain and we found high-grade ore. Even today, with all these men out here, no one bothers with low-grade ore, because there's still so much high-grade stuff all over. You go out to any hillside where you can stake a claim in that circle I told you

14

about, which is thirty miles across, and just dig into the side of the mountain until you hit ore. Don't bother with shafts or hoists or pumping plants or none of that stuff you need in other places. Here in the San Juan, you just scratch in the dirt like a chicken and you root up silver."

"How do I get the ore out to the smelter?" Raider asked.

"Same way as you came in."

"Over all those mountain passes?"

"I reckon it must be three hundred miles of hauling pay dirt by burro. The town of Mineral Point here is at an altitude of 11,700 feet, so the Army says, and I tell you that a man has to climb higher than that to get out of here."

Raider nodded. "I met strings of loaded burros going out on my way in."

"You have to mill the ore first to get rid of plain earth and dead rock in order to make each burro's load as much high-grade ore as you can."

"That's some goddamn journey out with loaded animals," Raider said.

The miner swallowed his whiskey. "It's worth it when you reach the smelters at the other end. Every bit of ore has been taken out by burro, from all the big mines—the Guston, Yankee Girl, Vanderbilt, Hudson, Mickey Breen, Pride of the West, Polar Star, Forest, Syracuse, Aspen, Red Roger, Ben Butler, Molas, Alaska, Silver Link, Old Lout. . . ."

Raider laughed and poured the miner more whiskey. "You sure can name them all."

"I could name another score of mines for you, and they would only be the big ones. Never worked on a big scale myself because I like to work alone. Lot of us old hands at the game are like that. Loners. We don't want to start no big-time operations like some of the newcomers here. Had a partner for a while a few years ago, but the Utes got him."

Raider said, "I heard there was a fellow in town, name

of Harrison, who had some idea for a new way of smelting right here in the mountains, so the burros could carry out almost pure silver instead of ore."

The miner's eyes widened. "So that's what he was up to. I seen him around the saloons every time I came to town for a while. I ain't never seen him out by the mines where men is workin'—he was always leaning on the bar of some saloon where people was up to no good. Little fella with a ginger mustache, acted like he was crazy half the time."

"That's him," Raider said.

"Ain't seen him in a while now," the miner said. "He must have moved on. I'd have heard about it if he got killed."

"Maybe he's working a strike somewhere."

The miner shook his head. "Naw. He wasn't no hard-scrabble miner. Is he a friend of yours?"

"Maybe."

The miner let that go. This big hombre who called himself Raider and who was generous with his whiskey was not the kind of person anyone demands answers from.

Raider had deliberately asked after the missing Arcady T. Harrison in a loud voice. The miner seemed to have nothing to hide. The bartender was another matter. As soon as Raider had mentioned the name Harrison, the bartender moved closer, polishing the bar top with a cloth, so he could hear every word Raider was saying to the miner. Raider might be rough-edged and not pay much attention to polite manners, but he was a trained observer as well as having a natural instinct for survival. He seemed to be unaware of the bartender eavesdropping on him and then going down the bar to talk in low tones to a man. They both looked back furtively along the bar at Raider from time to time.

When Raider paid for the whiskey consumed from his bottle and said goodbye to the miner he had been talking with, the other man followed him out the door and down the street, obviously believing that Raider hadn't noticed the bartender talking with him. Raider made his way through the bustling activities on the main street of the mining town. The man following Raider had difficulty keeping him in sight and had to trot now and then to keep up with the long strides of his quarry. Then Raider vanished.

His pursuer scanned the crowds on the street, peered into saloons and stores, looked up and down the street again, wandered into an alleyway between two buildings—

The first punch caught him in the nose, blinding him with his own tears and confusing him with pain and shock. The next blow he took was in the right ribs, knocking the wind out of him and making him forget the pain in his nose with the sharp new agony in his side. The third punch was surprisingly gentle, a wallop in the upper chest that sat him back on his ass in the dust.

The man groveled and wheezed on the ground at Raider's feet. When his right hand sneaked around to the handle of his six-gun, Raider cut him across the back of that hand with the spur of his left boot. The downed man sucked the blood from his hand and sank back, beaten.

"Where's Arcady T. Harrison?" Raider growled.

"I don't know." As he saw Raider's boot being drawn back for a kick, he raised his arm before his face and added quickly, "I swear I got no idea where Harrison is. That's what I'm being paid to do. Find him."

"Who do you work for?"

"Calvin Thornton."

"Never heard of him," Raider said.

"You will if you stick around town long enough. He's one of the biggest assayers in these parts. He buys a lot of silver from the San Juan mines."

"Do you know why your boss Thornton wants you to find Harrison?"

"He said this Harrison was working for some New York crowd who wants to steal his business. Look, I ain't going to say anything about you to Thornton, and you tell no one I told you I worked for him. I don't give a shit about any of this. I work for whoever pays me. I don't have no loyalties."

"I can see that," Raider commented and walked away from the cringing man.

Major W. D. Wheeler, the government Indian agent at the Uncompahgre Agency, stared in frustration at the big Ute seated in his office. The Indian was dressed in a frock coat, silk shirt and vest of excellent quality, combined with buckskin leggings and moccasins, gem necklaces, and long hair from which hung a single eagle feather. His deportment in the white man's office suggested the value he placed on his own dignity, physical presence, and power of confrontation.

The major was precise and businesslike, an ex-Army paymaster rather than a fighting man. "The Army is not coming into the San Juan to fight the Southern Utes," he explained, "but only to establish a fort from which your people will be able to get many wonderful things as gifts. Plows, for example. With plows you can till the fertile soil in valley bottoms and grow crops."

Chief Ouray spoke in a monotone. "When the land is plowed, it will no longer be Ute land."

Major Wheeler huffed with impatience. "Why not?"

"It will be white man's land, because this is what the white man does to the ground. And the Indians who plow the land will become white men. Their skins will grow pale and they will forget the sacred songs."

"Damn it, Ouray, you know as well as I do such talk is mumbo jumbo," the major expostulated. "You're every bit as intelligent a man as I am. Why can't you see how much better off you and your people all would be as Christians who live in houses and farm the land? Why do you chase off missionaries and live in those dirty old teepees?"

The Indian looked at the wall and said nothing.

Major Wheeler realized he had gone too far again. He accepted the fact that he lacked the personal charm and winning manner of his predecessor at the agency, the Reverend Henry F. Bond, and ordinarily it would not have mattered a whit whether the local Indians liked or disliked him. But in the San Juan it was different. The Utes made the miners and every other white man in the area constantly aware that but for Ouray's insistence that they go unharmed, none would live to see the sun rise on another day. Without Ouray's friendship, a wholesale massacre could begin at any moment.

The major decided to rephrase his comments. "What I meant to convey, Ouray, was that the benefits of our civilization can be yours at any time you choose to accept them. My job as government agent to your people is simply to make these options known to you."

"If the Army comes, we will fight."

The major looked amazed. "Who said anything about soldiers marching against you? They will come to help your people."

"Tell them we will fight."

The major gave in. "Very well. No soldiers. For now." He raised a finger in warning. "But if there's any big trouble, I won't be able to stop them coming in."

"No missionaries," the Indian added truculently.

"The government will provide protection for none—that's all I can promise. Any crazy enough to come here on their own—"

"We will drive them away."

"Good idea, Ouray. Much better than killing them."

"They do not deserve a warrior's death."

Major Wheeler looked oddly at the Ute chief. The fellow said the strangest things, and the major often could not make head or tail of them. This worried Wheeler. As an Army paymaster, he had been an efficient and just administrator. In the Army, things were spelled out clearly and a man knew what was expected of him. But this Indian agency was another kettle of fish entirely. The major still had no sure idea why Ouray permitted white men in the San Juan. His predecessor, the Reverend Bond, had some highfalutin notions about Ouray doing it because it pitted his will against those of all his fellow Utes. Thus, in the reverend's opinion, every white man a Ute saw in the San Juan was a living reminder to him of Ouray's power. No amount of great deeds could rival such a living display of power.

The major had a more straightforward account, if not explanation, of what had happened. In his view, the U.S. government had created its own monster in Chief Ouray. Since he had been the only Southern Ute chief with a good knowledge of English, the bureaucrats in Washington had treated him as a spokesman for his people—a role Ouray was pleased to assume. Apparently his fellow Utes had been less enthusiastic about Ouray's leadership than the government civil servants, a fact that Ouray had not translated into English for the white men. Using goods and the most modern guns supplied to him and his allies by the government, Ouray established a reign of terror through a series of murders and threats. Major Wheeler, retired now from the Army, found himself as Indian agent in his old role as paymaster. This time he was paying Ouray and his cronies with weapons, ammunition, and goods in exchange for "peace" in the San Juan.

Wheeler knew his job depended on his keeping Ouray happy. He suspected that the Ute chief knew this as well as he did.

"No soldiers, no missionaries," the major said.

"No plows," the Indian added, unappeased.

"No plows," the major confirmed. "And no attacks on the white man."

"White men are my closest friends," Ouray told him. "They are my brothers."

"Then what about Tahkoonicavats?" the major asked, referring to a rebel Ute subchief.

"He does not kill the white man."

"No, not with a gun or an arrow, he doesn't," the major agreed. "He just burns bridges, causes landslides and fires and sets traps so the white man can kill himself."

Ouray nodded approvingly.

"Do you know what the President in Washington says? He says Ouray is afraid of Tahkoonicavats and can't stop his plundering and destruction."

A look of great anger crossed the Ute chief's face.

"The President says that Ouray is his friend," the major went on, "and that he knows Ouray would stop this Ute, who is only a subchief, if he had the power to do so."

Ouray's face now wore a look of thunder.

Since the major was not quite sure whether the Ute chief was mad at him or Tahkoonicavats or maybe even the President, he decided to change the subject in order to avoid possible unpleasantness. Using unaccustomed diplomacy, the major avoided the matter of whiskey, which Utes were forbidden to drink by government regulations. The large quantities that they did consume they bought off suppliers to the miners with money provided to Ouray by the government. The Indians had no other use for the money and therefore associated it solely with whiskey. Ouray passed out money to friend and foe alike, to show how mighty he was—and thus the supply of firewater was under his control and liberally financed by Washington, which also forbade its use by Indians. The major had never been able to make Ouray understand this situation. He was no longer sure he really understood it anymore.

However, there was one disagreeable subject the major could not avoid bringing up, because he had been newly pressured about it from high levels.

"Have you seen Arcady T. Harrison?" the major asked the Ute chief.

"Who?"

"The man who is missing. He has important friends in New York. They say Ouray knows where he is."

"How do they know that?" Ouray asked.

"They are very clever men."

"They sound like stupid men to say a thing like that. Where are they? Bring them here."

"New York is too far away."

The Ute smiled. "That is why they dare say such a thing about me."

The Log Hill Mesa route was the shortest and most popular trail to the mines. In most places it rose in gradual ascents steep as a house roof. The uphill climb was made southward from the Uncompahgre country. The downhill side, fronting on Dallas Creek, was even steeper than the uphill. Loaded wagons often picked up so much speed on the descent, they could not be slowed.

Doc Weatherbee had just seen one such incident. The weight of two miners and an open wagon loaded down with supplies forced the four mules in harness downhill at an ever increasing pace until the mules were galloping headlong. One of the mules lost its footing, and the wagon slewed sideways and nearly went over a sharp drop into a creek hundreds of feet beneath. The animal regained its footing, and the load began to build up speed down the hill again— but this time the miners jumped clear. The four mules ran as hard as they could to try to keep ahead of their heavy burden pushing them from behind, until another of the animals stumbled and brought the entire team down upon its knees. The wagon smashed into the foundering animals, killing them instantly, and somersaulted down the hill, narrowly missing another wagon, before it shattered to pieces on the rocks and scattered its contents over the trail.

Doc spoke to Judith, his beloved mule, hitched to the wagon on which he was about to begin his own descent. "Take no mind of that, Judith. You and I are going to go down nice and easy. I'll look out that no one follows too closely on our heels, in case they crash into us. Nice and easy now, girl."

Judith did not budge.

"Come on, Judith," Doc pleaded. "We'll take it slowly."

The mule looked down the steep decline, twitched her ears, and dug her four hooves into the stony soil in truculent refusal.

A nearby miner laughed. "I'll be damned if this ain't the first time I've ever seen a mule look plain scared."

Doc stared back malevolently at Judith's insulter.

"Nothing personal, mister," the miner added. "It's just that I ain't never seen a mule before with a look like that on its face."

Doc had to laugh. "I guess you're right. Judith here is one smart mule and has her own opinions on just about everything. Right now, she doesn't believe a word I'm telling her."

The miner showed Doc how to hitch a heavy log to the hind axletree of his wagon to delay his descent. Apparently Judith approved of this device, because she agreed to move forward again next time Doc asked her to.

The medicine bottles rattled in their cases as the wagon began the steep descent on a trail that spiraled and swooped dizzyingly down the huge Colorado mountains. The trail at the summit had been bare rock colonized by lichens and moss. Farther down, hardy alpine plants—low, tough, and resilient—poked their leaves out of dirty snowbanks whose windblown remnants might just survive the summer. Below the snowline, conifers appeared. The high-altitude pines, spruce, and larch were stunted and twisted off to one side by their exposure to wind and cold. Below these came oak and aspen, and in the valleys, cottonwood and willows along the banks of clear mountain streams.

Doc Weatherbee looked over all this alpine splendor with the vague distaste of a city dweller worried about damage to his clothes. Every now and then he brushed the red trail dust off his suit, uncaring of the snickers this caused among the rough and ready miners who saw him. Most of them were dressed in thick, patched clothes and stank so high they claimed it frightened off bears.

A banner hung on each side of Doc's Studebaker wagon, proclaiming the rig to be that of DOCTOR WEATHERBEE—HOMEOPATHIC MEDICINES—FREE CONSULTATION. Doc had traveled for some years now in the guise of a homeopathic physician, using it as a cover for his activities as a Pinkerton operative. He had bought the wagon, along with Judith and its stock of medicines, from a physician in Carson City. Doc had not initially recognized the responsibilities he was undertaking in using the disguise of a doctor. He immediately found himself having to recommend cures to people in order to maintain his disguise. He read up on medical subjects and talked with genuine physicians until he worked out a course to follow. Stocking the wagon with harmless medicines only, he prescribed these for the imaginary ailments of the majority of his customers. Those unfortunates Doc suspected of being really ill he always found a way to send to a doctor with a college-earned diploma—not that he privately believed that this would do them much good, but it relieved him of the responsibility.

There were few places a doctor wasn't needed or welcomed, so in spite of the occasional complications, it was

an effective disguise for a Pinkerton to have. By degrees
Doc found himself becoming very fond of Judith—in fact,
if he had to drop the medical disguise, he suspected he
would find another which necessitated the use of the mule.

Doc's pharmaceutical supplies consisted of everything
from dried lizard skins and snake oil to Captain Dunphy's
Little Liver Pills, which promised to flush that organ completely clean—but which in Doc's opinion did nothing except leave a bitter taste in the mouth. He carried more than
a dozen guaranteed cures for the vapors, three for nocturnal
emissions, and nine for general biliousness. Doc had smiled
at first when he had handed out these medicines—until he
found that they really worked. It didn't matter much what
medicine he dispensed for which complaint, it was the act
of the patient taking the medicine that did the trick. Most
patients immediately started feeling better after taking a
powder or a pill or after applying some ointment. That was
when Doc began to realize that most illness is in the mind
and is best cured there. At times Doc tended to get carried
away and forget he was not a qualified physician—except
when he came across a case of real sickness. But he reckoned
that in the mountains of this part of Colorado, not a great
many people died of mysterious maladies in their beds. A
hell of a lot more died in the prime of health, with their
boots on.

After negotiating the steepest part down from the summit,
Doc unhitched the heavy log from the wagon's hind axletree
and let Judith find her way along the winding trail. He did
not pressure the mule, letting her move onward at her own
pace. As a result, his wagon was soon far behind the small
convoy with which he had set out from the summit.

The creaking of the wagon's wooden wheels over the
uneven trail masked the sound of horses' hooves behind
him. Doc swung about when he caught sight of the lead
horseman out of the corner of his eye. The man had ridden

up alongside the wagon before Doc had got a good look at him. He was an arrogant-looking man, prematurely white-haired, who rode stiffly upright on a bay stallion. His mustache was as white as his hair, and his eyes were blue, cold, and appraising. As well as riding a magnificent horse, his saddle was of the best craftsmanship, studded with Mexican silver designs, and his clothes were well tailored and cared for. Doc raised his derby in greeting and ran his eyes quickly over the three hombres accompanying the white-haired gentleman. The man snubbed Doc. The three drifters, saddle-weary and mean as sidewinders, looked over the nattily attired physician as if he had just called their mothers an ugly name.

Doc knew there would be trouble when the last one slowed his horse to the pace the mule was traveling and peered into Doc's face.

"What you say to me, fella?" the drifter demanded.

Doc looked back evenly into the bloodshot eyes in the unshaven, battered face. He asked in a very polite voice, "Are you speaking to me?"

"Listen to this fancy dude!" the drifter jeered. "You fast-talkin' scumbag, you ain't selling me none of your little bottles of colored water!"

"Why? What's wrong with you?" Doc asked with interest.

"Ain't nothing wrong with me," the drifter growled. "We're talking 'bout what's wrong with you."

"I feel fine, thank you," Doc said airily.

"You may not feel so good when I get done with you."

"Carter!" the white-haired man shouted back. "Leave the quack alone!"

"I'm just getting some medicine for what ails me, boss," the drifter shouted back with a crooked smile. He looked at Doc. "Man there is Mr. Calvin Thornton. One of the most important people hereabouts. You can thank your stars he was along to save you from me." He pulled a silver dollar from a vest pocket and handed it to Doc. "Give me something to feel good."

"What's wrong with you?"

"Nothin's wrong with me. Gimme something to feel loco."

Doc handed him a bottle containing a red liquid. The man drained it off in a single draft and tossed the empty bottle past Doc's right ear into the wagon. It landed with a tinkle of breaking glass.

The drifter gave Doc a long, hard look. "Stay out of my way when you see me coming."

Doc gave him a cheerful smile and said nothing.

The four horsemen were soon out of sight around a bend in the trail ahead, and Doc continued onward at his leisurely pace. He came upon them again after a while, three waiting by the trail and holding a horse with an empty saddle.

"What'd you give Carter?" one of the drifters yelled at Doc. "This is the fourth time he's had to go behind the bushes."

Doc said seriously, "He looked to me as if he were suffering from constipation."

The man laughed. "You sure cured him of that."

Doc Weatherbee flicked the reins and moved on. When they had met before, he had been beneath the proud, white-haired man's notice. This time he felt himself being carefully examined by the man Carter had called *Mr*. Calvin Thornton.

CHAPTER THREE

Ouray would one day like to meet the President who lived in Washington and see for himself if the man was as great as Wheeler claimed and worthy of his respect. That the President had never heard of him did not occur to Ouray. It seemed reasonable to Ouray that the great leader of the whites should think often about him, the great leader of the Southern Utes. Ouray had sometimes caught out Major Wheeler, the agent, in lies and had acted accordingly, but his overwhelming pride never allowed him to even question in his own mind whether the President had actually said the things Wheeler attributed to him. Ouray often thought about the President. He assumed that the President constantly thought about him too.

The President's taunt that he, Ouray, could not control the subchief Tahkoonicavats rankled because it was true. But not for the reasons the white man thought. Ouray did not physically fear the subchief and would have killed him long ago were it not for Tahkoonicavats' standing among his people. The guardians of the spirits and keepers of the tradition all backed him against Ouray, and Ouray knew that he could not fight invisible forces with lead bullets and steel blades.

The Ute medicine men feared that Ouray would finally permit Christian missionaries to come among them. They saw Tahkoonicavats as a defender of their interests, but dared not stand against Ouray so long as he too forbade white missionaries and soldiers. His killing of Tahkoonicavats would unite them against him openly, and unleash the powers of the spirit world against his every action. Ouray knew that the President in Washington similarly could not do things he would like to do for reasons perhaps like Ouray's own, and Ouray wished he knew the white man better to understand his ways in these matters. Major Wheeler was a fool and of no account. Ouray had long ago decided he would learn nothing of value from him. In the meantime he would have to fight the Ute medicine men on their own terms.

He had to find something that would terrify the guardians of the spirits and keepers of the tradition. This was what he was thinking about now. If his plan worked, no Ute would dare challenge his status as a great chief again.

A family member came to tell Ouray that two white miners had been shot and scalped. Ouray flew into a rage and rounded up his men for an attack on Tahkoonicavats. He now had the excuse he needed. Up to this time, the rebel subchief had restricted himself to being a nuisance by destroying and stealing—without ever challenging Ouray's authority directly. There could be no doubt about this: Killing and scalping two white men was meant as a personal insult to Ouray. He would have to avenge their deaths as if they had been members of his own family. The white men were in the San Juan because he, Ouray, said they could be there. They were his children. He was a very great chief.

Ouray took particular care to follow the sacred ritual in preparing for combat, remembering his uncertain relationship with the world of the spirits and not wishing to cause them any offense by hurrying or forgetfulness. Even when Ouray noticed a younger brother of Tahkoonicavats arrive at his encampment in the middle of a sacred war chant, his voice did not waver and his eyes stared fixedly in front of him. When the subchief's brother joined in the chant and in the dance to the war drum, Ouray began to wonder whether the spirits had begun to confront him in their own mysterious ways by making happen what he knew was not possible.

At the end of the chant, the subchief's brother greeted Ouray in a formal manner, praised him, and claimed that his brother had sent him to join Ouray's war party as a token of his support against those who had killed the two white miners.

Ouray would either have to accept his support or call Tahkoonicavats a liar by refusing it, implying that he still really believed that the subchief was responsible. Whatever the truth might ultimately be, Ouray knew that the subchief was too proud to lie to him except as part of an elaborate trick which people would have to admire for its originality and cleverness. Before the young man's speech was half over, Ouray had made up his mind. He would welcome him to his war party.

But now Ouray and his followers stood around painted and armed for war with nowhere to go. Ouray suggested a deer hunt, to be followed by a great feast and bottles of firewater. The warriors leaped on their horses and rode out of camp, eager to show their prowess as hunters.

Ouray ate little at the feast and drank no firewater. The two white men had been scalped as an insult to him. Was someone here secretly watching him and waiting for him to move, imagining himself to be the stalking panther and Ouray the foolish, timid goat? Ouray looked at the faces of the feasting and joking men and thought to himself: Let any one of them think himself a panther—it's when a rabbit imagines himself a panther that he is easiest to kill.

Midway through the feast, while the sun was still high, a boy from the group that summered highest on the slopes came with a message for Ouray. It was a challenge for

Ouray to meet man to man in a fight to the death at Turtle Bend.

There was great noise and tumult after the boy delivered this message in an uncertain voice. Ouray alone was calm. He told the boy to sit and eat. Knowing that all eyes were upon him only increased Ouray's resolution and calculation. Although the boy had called the challenger by his Ute name, Ouray liked to think of him by what the white man called him—Mr. Hot Stuff.

He had earned this name at Carlile Indian School by nearly blowing himself to pieces during a chemistry class there. Like Ouray, he was educated by the white man and therefore distrusted by his own people. Between the two men, however, their book learning deepened their rivalry. Ouray had run Mr. Hot Stuff off the reservation area twice, and Major Wheeler had followed this up by having him jailed once for two years. In Wheeler's words, Mr. Hot Stuff was one of "Uncle Sam's reservation tramps" and a "blanketed outlaw."

Ouray left the feast in a dignified manner, picked up his weapons, and rode off in the direction of Turtle Bend. The river here ended its run along a broad valley and formed a big pool before escaping into a narrow canyon between two hills. The hills were clad with evergreens, and the tall grasses of the valley stretched away undisturbed. The only moving creature Ouray could see as he sat on his horse atop a small elevation was a big hawk quartering the tall grass for its prey. He heard the distant rush of water in the canyon and the piping of birds in the trees. Everything was still. Too still. Unnaturally quiet.

He urged his mount on toward the edge of the pool, and he noticed the horse's nostrils dilate and twitch as they caught the scent of something. Another horse perhaps— no, there could be none near enough to be scented without also being seen. A man then. Concealed nearby in the tangle of willow saplings and rushes at the pool's edge.

Ouray smiled grimly to himself and felt his blood race and his mind swoop like a swallow low over the water. He urged his horse into the tangle of saplings and listened to the hollow sucking sounds its hooves made as they lifted out of the marshy ground. He might die today. Why not? Who could say that it would not be better to leave life now, at this instant, rather than wait till tomorrow or some other day? He might not be ready at all to meet death then. As he was now. At this moment, with his mind and blood afire, he could face anything and suppress fear.

His mind saw them before his eyes—the yellow flowers on the branches of a small bush which children picked to show their mothers. Ouray himself had picked them as a small child. He did not remember the plant's name, but he did remember it grew on high, stony ground, never in low marshy places like this. He slipped his knife blade free of its buckskin sheath.

As his horse neared the yellow-flowered bush, he saw it move ever so slightly—not as a breeze moves a branch but a small tense movement. Ouray eased his horse's head a little to the left, so that he came upon the bush on his right side. His breath was fast and shallow, his heart beat wildly, and his right hand tightly clutched the knife handle as he neared the bush.

The flowered bush shot upward out of the tangle of willow saplings, and two arms and clutching hands reached for him to pull him from his horse. Ouray drove the knife blade straight down with all his strength. He felt the steel puncture flesh, scrape against bone, and plunge all the way in. A surge of warm blood covered his right hand to the wrist, and the pair of hands clutching at him weakened and fell away.

Ouray dismounted and pulled away the flowered bush that was tied to the back of the dying man, concealing his head and shoulders. It was not Mr. Hot Stuff, but a friend of his, another outcast of the Utes. The chief remained squatting down, hearing the irregular gasps and moans of the dying man. Ouray's eyes scanned all about him for a movement or any object out of its natural place. Nothing caught his eye. He cleaned his bloody knife on the grass and resheathed it. Then he rose and walked toward his horse.

A figure emerged from the saplings some distance away. Ouray dove for cover as a bullet whistled over him and he heard the crack of a rifle shot. He crawled on his belly toward his horse, which was rearing in panic at the shot. A second shot caused the horse to bolt, and along with it went Ouray's two rifles in their saddle sheaths.

The rifleman now advanced through the saplings over the marshy ground. Ouray crawled back to his previous attacker, who was now dead. The man had no rifle. Ouray took his revolver. He now had two revolvers, but he was still no match for a rifleman, who could stay just out of pistol range and shoot till he picked him off. Ouray saw the rifleman's features. It was Mr. Hot Stuff. Cold rage spread through Ouray at the way his opponent had played a cowardly trick on him by bringing along a hidden ally after challenging him to a man-to-man fight to the death. Truly, Ouray reasoned, even if the members of the spirit world were annoyed with him because of what he did, they must now be even more disgusted with Mr. Hot Stuff—or at the very least would not take his side in this challenge.

Ouray made his way on his hands and knees to the water's edge. Bullets whistled over his crawling form, and as Mr. Hot Stuff closed the distance between them, his accuracy was improving. He seemed to have plenty of ammunition and forced Ouray to keep as close to the ground as a weasel. The chief cut a hollow cane the length of his arm by the edge of the pool and eased himself into the water.

He swam hardly at all, barely moving his arms and legs

to keep himself afloat, with as little of his head out of the water as he could manage and still breathe. The slow current in the big pool carried him along, and the icy mountain water chilled his body.

The splash of a ricocheting bullet rose near his face, followed by another on the other side of his head. Mr. Hot Stuff had run to the riverbank and was now trying out his marksmanship on the bobbing target of Ouray's head. He would have plenty of time to do so.

Ouray put the hollow cane in his mouth and completely submerged. His waterlogged clothes helped keep his body floating just beneath the surface of the water while he breathed with his mouth through the hollow cane, whose tip extended above the surface. As he drifted along on his back, Ouray opened his eyes underwater and saw one bullet bounce off the surface directly above his face.

The current quickened gradually, and Ouray felt himself being swept along with increasing speed. Yet he dared not surface, because he guessed that Mr. Hot Stuff was running along the bank, hoping for another shot.

Before Ouray had much time to think more about his predicament, the water decided things for him. The river water now held him in its fingers like a soft, giant, invisible hand, turning him this way and that, so that he rolled and sucked in a mouthful of water instead of air through the hollow cane. He choked and coughed bubbles, broke the surface with his head, and gasped for air.

The water was turbulent all about him, fleeting over the smooth bare rocks with frightening speed. Instead of willow and marshy banks, gaunt rock cliffs rose on either side. Things grew darker as he was swept more deeply into the canyon, and the roar of the water and its echoing inside the steep rock walls terrified him. He tried to thrash out for shore, but there was no shore—just sheer slippery walls of cold rock and almost total darkness now except for a narrow ribbon of light hundreds of feet above him, which was the peaceful blue sky. The roar of the water grew still louder, and he almost cried out in pain as a chute of water dragged his body across a coarsely crystalline rock. He felt himself traveling faster. . . .

Raider knew he was getting nowhere with the punctilious military man but tried once again. "Major Wheeler, if Arcady T. Harrison isn't in Mineral Point or one or the other mining towns, and if he isn't out at one of the mines—I've checked, and he isn't at any of those places—where else could he be if he's still alive except out among the Utes?"

The major nodded that he followed this line of reasoning, yet said nothing.

Raider went on, "Now, if there's one white man who might know what's going on out there with the Utes, it's the Indian agent, right?"

The major nodded once again and maintained his silence.

"Major, you happen to be the Indian agent hereabouts. So I'm asking you on behalf of my dear cousin and lost friend, Arcady T., have you any idea where he might be?"

"You're a Southerner, Mr. Raider?"

"Yes, sir. My daddy fought with the Confederates. I'd have fought too if I was old enough."

Major Wheeler sniffed with disapproval. "Mr. Harrison, to the best of my knowledge, had no relatives south of the Mason-Dixon line."

Raider smiled sadly. "He never spoke of us to nobody. I guess he was ashamed of us, us being poor and ignorant and all, while he was such a genius. He didn't want us dragging him down."

Major Wheeler slapped his palm on his desk. "This is pure effrontery, sir! How dare you present me with such cock-and-bull stories! If I were still in the Army, I'd have you taken off to cool your heels awhile."

Raider looked hurt. "Are you saying that you don't believe me?"

"I'm saying more than that, sir! I'm saying that your story is preposterous and that you plainly have some other ulterior motive in looking for Mr. Harrison."

Raider knew he was beaten. He produced his identification. "I'm a Pinkerton."

The ex-Army man looked over the identification papers suspiciously at first, then raised his head with a friendly smile. "Well, this puts a different complexion on things. Up to this, I thought you were one of those gunmen hired by Cal Thornton."

"Everyone seems to be looking for Harrison," Raider commented. "I hear Thornton was afraid Harrison would put him out of business."

"That's not exactly how I heard it," the major responded. He produced a bottle of whiskey and two glasses from a desk drawer. "One of the bad habits I learned in the Army— I was one of the few who had a desk to hide a bottle in. What I heard about Thornton and Harrison was this: Cal paid him to go in with him instead of the New York people who originally sent him here. That would be typical of Thornton. I remember him years ago up in the Montana Territory— he had a contract to supply the Army with food. He was pretty good at it too, if I remember rightly. No more honest than anyone else, I suppose, but the Army cared less about that than dependability. Thornton never let us down. Now he's the biggest assayer and smelter in these parts. Most of the burro trains you see leaving here are on their way to his assaying office. Miners say he's fair and square with them. They bitch like hell about some of the other assayers, but I've heard nothing bad about Thornton. Not that I like the man much personally. He's a haughty son of a bitch. But I can't complain. He's done me no wrong."

Raider was amazed at the sudden change in the personality of the major. At first he had thought Wheeler just naturally cold and cagey. But after the major had seen Raider's Pinkerton papers, Raider couldn't shut him up. It was as if the ex-Army man was starved for conversation with someone who represented authority—although a Pinkerton operative did not quite fit in that category, and certainly Raider least of all.

Raider let him ramble on before putting questions to him.

"You think Ouray's disappearance has anything to do with Harrison's?"

"No, I don't," Major Wheeler replied. "Ouray is famous for calling down other Ute warriors in duels to the death and killing them in hand-to-hand combat. Have you seen his wife Chipeta? She's very beautiful. Her brother, Sapinero, tried to murder Ouray with an ax at the Cochetopa Agency. Ouray overpowered him, knelt above him, and was about to cut the heart out of his living body slowly with his knife when the beautiful Chipeta arrived and pleaded for her brother's life. Ouray let him go unharmed, and he and Chipeta have been together since."

"That's one way to meet a wife," Raider observed.

"There's a whole list of other warriors who didn't have beautiful sisters to arrive at the last minute to save their hides. Ouray has killed Suckett, Dynamitz, Jack of Clubs, Lucifer, who was also known as Old Nick—"

"Are these Utes?"

"Sure. But they have these long unpronounceable Indian names, most of 'em, so the ones who get known to us, we give 'em names we can remember and pronounce."

Raider said nothing, but he could guess what the Utes thought about this particular Indian agent.

"No, I don't think Ouray's disappearance is connected with that of Harrison," the major went on. "I know that Ouray got called down by Mr. Hot Stuff, who seemingly

was the one who killed the two miners. All I know is that
they found another dead Indian where the fight was to have
taken place at Turtle Bend, and Ouray's horse returned home
without him. He hasn't been seen since then, whereas Mr.
Hot Stuff has."

"Sounds like Ouray has fought his last fight."

"I agree," the major said. "Yet I have my suspicions.
He's a clever, devious man. When I went looking for Harrison myself, as I was asked to do by Washington, Ouray
was certainly one of two people who I thought might know
where he was."

"Who was the other?"

"Laura Winton," the major said. "I bet you've noticed
her. She's a . . . well, you know—she hangs out in saloons.
A tall, thin woman, beautiful in her way, I suppose, but a
bit wild-looking and fierce for my taste. She likes to make
a lot of noise and is a damn fine poker player."

Raider nodded. "I've seen her."

"She and Harrison were inseparable for a while—at least
while he happened to be in town, which was more often
than not. They made quite a pair. She was so tall and he
was so short. He seemed to have lots of money and was
very generous with it."

"Did he ever talk about the new smelting process he was
supposed to be working on?"

"All the time," the major said. "He promised to save all
the miners a lot of work and make everyone rich. They
were interested at first. But when they saw he was spending
most of his time in the saloons with Laura instead of at the
mines, they decided he was just another smart-talkin' Easterner who didn't want to get dirt under his fingernails."

"You figure Laura knows where Arcady T. Harrison is
now?" Raider asked.

"She wasn't telling me whether she did or not. But then
I'm not the best person to talk with a sporting woman like

that. Especially when she's taller than me. You might do better."

Raider stroked his mustache and flexed his biceps. "No harm in me trying, I guess."

"I wish you luck. I want this Harrison fellow to be found as much as you do. It doesn't make me look good when a white man with powerful connections back east disappears in Ute country. And I think a lot of that money Harrison was spending was Cal Thornton's—so Thornton might be a big help to you also in searching for Harrison."

"You been real helpful, Major. I appreciate that. I know you'll keep it to yourself about me being a Pinkerton."

"I'll tell no one."

"I've one last question. Did Arcady T. Harrison do anything out of the ordinary, no matter how trivial, before he disappeared?"

The major thought for a moment, then smiled in recollection. "Funny you should mention it, but he did. He was a real eccentric. Harrison ordered in a mysterious shipment of merchandise by burros and brought it out of town soon after it arrived. It so happened Harrison wasn't about when the burros first got into town, and one of the stable lads was curious and looked into some of the barrels. Know what was inside? Paper! Thousands of sheets of it—that fine brown manila paper that high-class stores use for parcels. Not your cheap grocer's variety."

"Nothing else?" Raider asked.

"Just fine brown paper. The man was losing his sanity, in my opinion."

"Maybe," Raider said, and left.

Raider noted Doc Weatherbee's arrival in Mineral Point without approaching him, since the two could probably work better without it being known there was a link between them—and certainly without it being known they were

Pinkertons. Some of the crazy youths toting guns would try to kill a Pinkerton for no better reason than to build a reputation as a killer. Other gunmen had scores to settle with the agency, and in their eyes the only good Pinkerton was a dead Pinkerton.

Seeing Doc arrive was a relief to Raider in one way, because he now knew he had a skilled, dependable partner on hand, but it was also an irritation in another way. Doc riled Raider too often, gave him a hard time, was always pulling his big-city stuff, lording it over him like he was somehow better than Raider. This time Raider had been doing fine on his own. He didn't need Doc's help on this case. He'd made a lot of progress. Now he'd be expected to share what he knew with Doc, and Doc would pull some clever con game on him and act like it was he who was the real field operative while Raider was only some kind of roustabout.

Still, Raider knew better than to let personal resentment interfere with his professional work—his job was too dangerous to allow that to happen. If a Pinkerton in the field wanted to stay healthy, he had to use every advantage he had and every bit of aid he was offered. Personal feelings didn't come into it.

Doc lodged Judith in the town stables and made his way to the only hotel, which was also the only two-story building in the town. The rest of the buildings ranged from canvas tents on wooden platforms to keep the mud out, all the way through cabins of pine logs and hovels of rough-hewn planks, to well-carpentered houses and stores owned by those who had struck it rich to some extent—or at least had hung on to what they had earned. The saloons likewise ranged from canvas-covered temporary structures with rotgut whiskey all the way up to three that sported gleaming brass, stained-glass windows, gaming tables, mirrors, and chandeliers—the Silver Spur, Hellgate Hanna's, and the Hotel San Juan.

In these three class establishments, miners were expected to arrive in clean clothes. Shaving and wearing a gun were optional.

Raider had a small back room on the second floor of the Hotel San Juan. Doc got himself a large corner room at the front of the second floor, with a view of the street from its tree-shaded balcony. Raider's room was directly above the bar and gaming tables, so that he was woken at odd hours by altercations going on beneath. Doc's was above the hotel office, was quiet and well furnished, and had a large double bed with a canopy.

All this was taken in by Raider as he briefed Doc on developments in the case so far.

Doc's only comment was, "I thought you'd have found Arcady T. Harrison by now."

"Too bad I had to disappoint you, Doc."

"Never mind. Now that I'm here, we'll find him without any more delay."

As Raider was about to explode, Doc grinned and passed him an unopened bottle of good bourbon. Raider's mind was immediately distracted from his grievances. They agreed to meet in Doc's room as necessary, but otherwise to pretend to be unacquainted. Doc would take a tour of the town that night, and Raider would cover him and indicate anything he should pay particular attention to.

"Like Laura Winton?" Doc asked.

"I tried with her and got nowhere," Raider said. "Maybe she likes runts like Harrison and you more than she likes real he-men."

Doc tut-tutted. "Sounds like that woman has no taste, turning down a fine stud like you. Must be something wrong with her. I reckon I don't stand a chance if she didn't fall for you."

Raider knew he was being baited and said nothing.

They ate separately in the hotel dining room and went

first to the hotel saloon. Things were quiet there, so they drifted up the street to the Silver Spur, Raider getting there maybe twenty minutes before Doc. He was standing at the bar, drinking with some miners he knew, and didn't see Doc come in.

As soon as Doc walked through the door, an unshaven character with a battered face, who looked like a hired gun going fast to seed, bellowed and stumped forward to meet Doc, hand hovering over his gun handle.

"Git the hell outta here! You carrying a gun, you goddamn snake-oil merchant? You near killed me out there on the Log Hill Mesa trail."

Doc ignored the man and walked past him.

Thus belittled in everybody's eyes, the man pulled his gun but couldn't shoot Doc in the back before all these witnesses. He waited till Doc turned toward the bar and put a quick shot into the floorboards in front of him.

"Dance for me, ye blasted varmint!" he shouted at Doc, and loosed off two more shots at his feet.

One bullet went clean through a floorboard a few inches from Doc's left foot, and the second bounced up off the floor, whistled past the head of an alarmed miner, and buried itself high in the saloon wall.

The crowd about the bar evaporated except for Doc Weatherbee, who stood his ground and had not budged his feet since being ordered to dance by the gunman, and Raider, who finally noticed that it was his partner who was in trouble.

"You heard me, possum scum," the gunman rasped, thumbing back the hammer of his six-gun. "I want to see you dance."

Raider's gun hand moved fast as a rattler striking a prairie dog. The Remington .44 spat flame and lodged a bullet in the floorboard between the gunman's boots.

The gunman rolled his bloodshot eyes over in the direction of this new combatant, who stood with a waft of blue smoke rising from his gun barrel. The gunman didn't make a move.

"This ain't no business of your'n," he growled at Raider.

"Seems to me this dude here"—Raider nodded in Doc's direction—"ain't wearing a gun. If you want to lay down your gun and use your fists on him, I won't interfere. I just like to see a guy get an even chance, no matter who he is."

The gunman's left hand went to the buckle of his gunbelt and his right hand began returning his pistol to its holster. Raider relaxed—almost. As the gunman was about to holster his weapon, instead he suddenly whipped it, still cocked, in Raider's direction and squeezed the trigger.

Raider stepped sharply to the left to avoid the bullet and fanned two shots at the gunman's midriff. The bullet aimed at Raider passed him and smashed a mirror behind the bar into small fragments. Raider's first slug caught his opponent square in his protruding belly, making a hollow thump like a rap on a heavy wood door and doubling him up, so that the second piece of lead entered through the crown of his hat.

He collapsed on the floor of the saloon. The way the blood was leaking through the crown of his hat and his open staring eyes were enough to tell the end of his story.

Raider stayed where he was, smoking gun in hand, eyeing five hombres who had lined up to oppose him on the other side of the saloon, with the dead body stretched between Raider and them. Raider had three shots left—he knew that Doc, like a damn fool, was probably unarmed as usual—but he had his gun drawn, and all five of them had to reach for theirs. He would take at least two, a good chance he'd take three, before they got him. He was sure of this. So were they. So they eyed him back, hanging loose, waiting for a good move.

Customers were scattering in real earnest now, barreling

out through the batwing doors into the street, two at a time. The outward flow eased for a moment in respect for the white-haired man with cold blue eyes who pushed his way in. He looked for a moment at the face-off and then walked over to the five men lined up in front of Raider.

Calvin Thornton spoke with them for a good two minutes while Raider watched with calm vigilance, the big Remington .44 steady and gleaming in his right hand.

Doc spent the time reknotting his necktie and checking out his appearance in a wall mirror.

With surly nods to Thornton, the five men approached the body sprawled on the floor and avoided looking in Raider's direction. They carried the body among them out the batwing doors.

"All right, folks," Thornton shouted. "It's all over. Come back in. A drink on the house for every man here!"

That was all the customers needed to hear. In seconds the place was back to normal, wth crowds striving at the bar for free booze.

Thornton approached Raider with a glossy smile. "Silver Spur is my place. I'll take care of this with the marshal. Won't be any problem in this town."

"You don't seem too upset at losing one of your men," Raider said warily.

"Carter was a troublemaker. I don't need troublemakers on my payroll—there's enough real trouble comes a man's way without his creating it. What are you doing in town? If you don't mind me asking."

"Passing through."

"I guessed so," Thornton said in a friendly way. "Maybe you'd do a small job for me while you're here?"

"I don't come cheap."

Thornton placed a twenty-dollar gold piece on the bar counter before Raider.

"What do you want me to do?" Raider asked.

"You been talking to that fancy quack you saved from Carter?"

Raider shook his head. "I never seen him before."

"Get to talking with him. He sold Carter a dose of something that gave him the runs real bad. That's why Carter was after him. You couldn't know that, of course. But I don't care about none of that. I think this quack may be in town for some reason other than helping folks get well. There's something funny about him. I don't trust him. You find out what he's here for and I got another twenty-dollar gold piece for you. Interested?"

"You got it."

Thornton winked at Raider.

Raider winked back.

CHAPTER FOUR

Doc Weatherbee spent all the next day making rounds of the mining camps. After leaving the town stables, on a lonely stretch where he knew there would be no prying eyes, he pulled aside some of the crates of medicine, released a concealed catch, and raised some of the floorboards of the wagon. He checked through the contents of the hidden compartment. There were two Gatling machine guns, pistols and rifles, ammo, explosives, telegraph equipment—which would be useless here in the mountains, since no lines had been strung—a camera and photographic supplies, and other items a traveling physician would not be expected to carry. Judith was rested and well fed, and thus was willing to cover a good deal of ground.

More interested in learning the lay of the land around Mineral Point than in finding out anything particular, Doc returned in late afternoon, satisfied with his day's effort. As always he talked with the stablemen, aware that they usually knew more about the comings and goings of people than anyone else in town. He listened to a lot of spicey gossip items about folks he had never laid eyes on or even heard of before, and in the middle of it brought up the subject of the crazy inventor whose name he could not rightly recall at that moment.

The stableman heard him sure enough but went right on talking without acknowledging it. Whether the man was

46

hiding· something or had simply grown weary of people asking him questions about Arcady T. Harrison, Doc could not tell, and he decided not to press the point. After making sure that Judith had fresh straw and an ample supply of oats and water, he patted the mule on the neck and made his way along the dusty and rutted main street to his room at the Hotel San Juan.

The mountain air had tired him, and he was resting on his bed when he heard a loud rap on the door.

"It's open," he called.

Raider came in, looked in disgust at the canopy over the bed, and went without a word for the bottle of Doc's good bourbon on a side table.

"Sell any of your medicine?" Raider finally asked in a sour tone.

"Yes, I did." Doc then went on to list his sales and discuss the medical symptoms until Raider couldn't stand it any longer.

"Shut up!"

"I thought you were interested, Raider."

"I'm not now. Did you find anything on Harrison?"

"Not a thing. And you?"

"I was looking for Mr. Hot Stuff. Since Ouray and Harrison have clean disappeared, maybe I can find out something from him. He's around all right, but very few of the Utes I came across understood what I was saying. I tried English on them and then all the bits and pieces of various Indian tongues I've picked up. They couldn't understand anything, or at least they pretended they couldn't. One old man—he must have been near a hundred—spoke good English and just laughed at me when I told him I was looking for Mr. Hot Stuff. He said the only way I would find him was to go around saying bad things about him, then I'd meet up with him soon enough. I asked about saying good things, but the old guy seemed to think that wouldn't work as well as insults. I told him that very few Utes understood anything I said, and he replied that Mr. Hot Stuff speaks very good English. He also said that if I shouted bad things about Mr. Hot Stuff here in Ute country, the rocks would hear me and tell him. That sounds crazy now, but I tell you for the rest of the day, as I shouted curses and things about Mr. Hot Stuff, I had the strangest feeling the rocks *were* listening to me. A real eerie feeling. . . ."

Raider had expected Doc to make fun of him for this, but instead Doc seemed genuinely interested.

"What names did you call him?" Doc asked.

"Bastard, son of a bitch, murderer, anything I could think of. Then I started to figure that maybe Mr. Hot Stuff might be complimented by being called things like that. So I called him *Miss* Hot Stuff for a while. I got back into town kind of hoarse and feeling like a fool."

"Going after Mr. Hot Stuff like you did was a good idea," Doc assured him.

Raider went to the door. "I'll see you later at the Silver Spur. Reckon I'll try to investigate what you're doing in town and earn myself another twenty dollars."

"Don't forget to report that income to Allan Pinkerton," Doc warned.

Later at the Silver Spur, Raider made a show of buying Doc drinks and talking with him. He even introduced Doc to Laura Winton—not because he wanted to but because Laura walked up to him and asked who Doc was. Doc took over from there.

Laura's tall, thin body was squeezed into a tight-fitting gown that showed off her breasts, shapely hips, and long thighs. She had a slinky walk and denied no man the pleasure of admiring her body's attractions. Her auburn hair tumbled down over her bare shoulders, and her melting brown eyes were as innocent as those of a meek and pure schoolgirl.

Her voice gave her away. It was harsh and nasal, and startled people when they first heard her talk because it was so much at odds with her appearance. Laura didn't give a damn what they thought.

"Sure," she purred to Doc. "There are only two kinds of men in the world—those with money and those without. Which kind are you?"

"Dedication to my profession," Doc informed her in a dignified tone, "demands that I leave the comforts of my mansion in Manhattan in order to bring life-saving medicines to the inhabitants of this godforsaken region."

She laughed in his face. "I guess there is a third kind of man in the world—those with bullshit instead of money."

They talked on for a little while, and then Doc suggested that although it was early in the evening, they might take a little rest in his hotel room. Laura was immediately agreeable. They left the Silver Spur and walked down the street together to the Hotel San Juan.

As soon as they were in Doc's room, Laura began to wriggle out of her tight gown. Her body was so curvaceous, she needed nothing like stays to create her shape. She just peeled off the dress and revealed bare skin.

Dressed only in black stockings and high heels, she walked across the room to a mirror and checked her hair, then took a few turns around the room so Doc could admire her naked body and savor its sinuous lines as she moved. Occasionally she glanced in his direction to make sure his eyes were upon her. She was not disappointed.

"Know what I feel like when I do this for a man?" she asked. "A good horse. You know how they walk 'em round and round in a ring so the buyers can get a good look at 'em?"

"You've got a fine pair of haunches," Doc remarked judiciously.

"Yeah, that's the kind of thing they say about horses all right. You might even find a horse with a better pair of haunches than I got. But one thing you won't find is a horse with tits like these."

Doc shucked off his clothes and went after her. She pressed her body provocatively against his and pushed her tongue into his mouth. Then she stood back to see what effect she had on him. Doc was left standing with his prick poking into the air, while she waltzed about him saying she had changed her mind and now didn't want to go to bed with him.

Doc said calmly, "I hear you're a friend of Arcady T. Harrison."

She got flustered, hesitated, then ran to him, pressed herself to him, clutching him tightly in her arms, and slipped her tongue into his mouth again.

This time Doc did not let her get away from him and steered her, step by step, toward the bed. His desire got the better of him before they reached the bed, however. He lifted her up by her rear cheeks so that her crotch was higher than the upstanding tip of his cock and then he slowly lowered her till he could feel the juicy lips of her sex part to admit his throbbing member.

He continued to lower her body, inch by inch, impaling her gradually on his engorged organ. He felt his cock slip all the way to the hilt into her warm slippery crevice as she wrapped her legs about his waist and locked her feet behind his back.

Laura Winton was a little flushed and her eyes sparkled brightly when she reentered the Silver Spur later that evening. She came in alone and sat at a table by herself, ignoring several offers of drinks and friendship. She placed a cigarette in a long holder and lit it, held it daintily in one gloved hand, and studied the patterns of the ascending smoke. When that cigarette burned out, she lit another.

She appeared to pay no heed when Doc Weatherbee came in through the batwing doors. He walked to the long bar without noticing her and was greeted by the big naive gunman called Raider who had introduced them. This was the second time she had seen Raider buying drinks for Doc. Why? Laura decided that Raider must be sick, and instead of facing the problem head on, in typical male fashion he was trying to drink it away in the company of a doctor rather than seeing him as a patient. Laura prided herself on being able to classify men almost at a glance — she had to be able to do so in her line of work, which was whoring and card-playing. One big mistake could be a girl's last mistake.

However, Doc puzzled her. He wasn't quite the traveling physician he at first appeared to be. And those questions about Arcady T. Harrison . . . Why did he want to know?

Laura remained alone, aloof to all offers, until a scruffy miner walked right up to her table and sat next to her without a word. The man's small frame, unkempt hair, and a week's growth of ginger beard was in strong contrast to the tall, elegant woman dressed in the latest fashion whom he sat beside. Yet Laura seemed extremely pleased with her new-found company.

"Arcady," she whispered. "They'll be bound to recognize you."

"They haven't before, and they won't this time either," the small man said with energy and confidence. "They're all looking for a talkative eastern intellectual, not an ungroomed miner in tattered clothes. The best disguise of all is not to change the color of your hair or shape of your nose, but simply to behave differently from what is expected. The man they're looking for would never be so foolish as to do what I'm doing now. This couldn't be me."

Laura smiled. "It's worked for you so far. You see that handsome, well-dressed man talking to the gunman called Raider who was asking about you before? Well, he's been asking about you too. I had him up to bed this evening— he's great, we had a lot of fun—and he didn't start asking questions until we had all our clothes off. Every time he asked, I stuck my tongue or a nipple in his mouth."

"Whore," Harrison said mildly.

"He never got an answer to his questions," Laura boasted. "Ain't you worried who he might be?"

"What does it matter? They all want to steal from me."

Laura was a bit put out at his lack of gratitude for her efforts on his behalf. "He's real handsome and a great lover. I might have been tempted to tell him about you. Don't you worry I might do that? If he offered me money?"

"I assumed he had."

"Trouble with you, Arcady, is you take me for granted."

Harrison smiled at her and held her hand under the table. "Every man needs a woman he can depend on."

"It doesn't hurt to say thank you now and then."

"Thank you."

She bought them drinks, and they stayed for a while.

"You feel like coming back to my room?" she asked.

"Fine by me."

"That's what I mean! You're the one who's supposed to ask! You just assume I'll be there to do everything for you. And you stink!"

"I've been working in the hot sun. Day after day."

"All right," she said. "Come along. I'll heat water, and you can have a nice bath. I might even help you."

They left the saloon together.

"That woman has strange taste in men," Raider commented. "First you, now him."

"Hang in there, Raider," Doc told him. "She'll get around to you yet."

Raider scowled. "You found out nothing from her about Harrison?"

"No." He added, "She was too excited by me physically to answer questions. She was so hot she didn't even listen."

Raider laughed disbelievingly yet with a look of envy.

Doc asked, "What've you got in mind for tonight?"

A more satisfied look crossed Raider's face. "I'm thinking of collecting that other twenty dollars from Calvin Thornton."

"That might make for an interesting evening," Doc commented. "You'll find me back at the hotel saloon—just in case anybody might be looking for me."

Doc left, and Raider whiled away the time with a few hands of poker. As usual, he lost. He was saved by the arrival of Thornton. Raider got up from the card table and pointedly went to the quiet end of the bar and kept to himself. Thornton did not keep him waiting.

"It'll cost you twenty," Raider said by way of a greeting.

The gold coin was slapped on the bar counter in front of him.

"This Doc Weatherbee," Raider said in response, "is looking for a missing inventor called Arcady T. Harrison. He says he's working for New York City investors who bought some kind of smelting process that Harrison thought up and is developing out here. Funny thing, though, this Weatherbee is no hired gun and he doesn't even act like an investigator. Know what I think he is? One of the investors themselves. He thinks he's got guts. This is his big adventure in the wilderness. My guess is that he aims to show the other fat cats back in New York that he can go out and do a real man's job as well as any mean hombre."

"You sure about this?" Thornton asked. "About him actually being one of the investors?"

"I can't be a hundred percent sure. He didn't come right out and tell me. But he slipped a few times by saying 'our' and 'my' money when he was talking about their investment in Harrison, and, like I said, no one would hire a dude like that to search for anything more valuable than a stray cat."

Thornton's cold eyes watched Raider. "You got more brains than I thought, big fella. You need work around here, just state your terms."

"'Preciate that."

"Give me an hour," Thornton said. "Then send word to Weatherbee that you want to meet him outside Shultz's Hardware Store. Don't show up."

Raider nodded, and Thornton left in a hurry.

Doc Weatherbee stopped off at the stables and, while no one was looking, fetched his .38 Diamondback pistol from the wagon's secret compartment, along with ammunition. He visited Judith and checked on her supply of oats. After loading and concealing the gun beneath his jacket, he set out for the hotel saloon. Doc rarely carried a gun, except when things got serious.

After an hour in the Hotel San Juan saloon, Raider still had not shown up and Doc began to get concerned. He could always depend on Raider for backup in a difficult situation—at least he had been able to up until now. Something must be wrong. Otherwise Raider would definitely have shown by this time.

"Message for Doc Weatherbee! Dr. Weatherbee!" a youth wandered about the saloon shouting, and the barman pointed to Doc.

"Mr. Raider says to meet him outside Shultz's Hardware Store."

"Where's that?"

"Lower end of town, sir. Heck of a place to meet you. All stores are closed down in that part of town at this time. No lights or nothin' down there now. I could guide you for a quarter."

Doc almost said yes until he realized he could be unfairly putting the youth in danger. He gave him the quarter anyway and set out into the night alone, having patted his pistol to make sure it was in place.

He stumbled a few times as he made his way in the dark over ruts gouged by wheels of loaded wagons in the dirt street. Taking his time, allowing his eyes to become accustomed to the dark, Doc made his way between the gray shapes of houses that loomed out of the night. Not a single light shone in any of the windows, for in this town most people, like the birds, went to sleep at dusk and rose at first light—except for the hell-raisers and loose-livers who hung around the saloons at the other end of town. This end was quiet as a graveyard.

Doc kept wondering why Raider had arranged to meet him down here, whether it was a joke or a trap. Where was Raider? Doc had one sure way to find out—keep going till he reached Shultz's Hardware Store. He eased out the .38 Diamondback from beneath his jacket and walked as silently as he could. By now his eyes could readily discern the shapes of the houses against the night sky, and his ears listened for the slightest scrape or pad that would indicate he was not alone in the street. He heard nothing but his own breathing and his soft footfalls on the dry dirt as he made his way carefully through the darkness.

He peered up at the false fronts of stores and tried to make out the names written on them. None looked as if it might be Shultz's, and anyway Raider was not outside any of them waiting for him. Not that he really expected to find Raider waiting for him. Without a doubt, this had to be some sort of trap. Whoever set it for him must have a low estimate of his intelligence to think that he would walk into it unknowingly. Yet here he was walking into it! But knowingly. And that made all the difference. He hoped.

Anyway he had no choice. He had to find Raider.

The looming bulk of the silent houses seemed oddly sinister in the silence of the night. Doc held his pistol ready and advanced slowly into the unknown.

Light suddenly flooded onto the street from a window of a shack on Doc's left, leaving him silhouetted on the street in a pale yellow glow. All Doc saw was a man's black-haired arm and hand place a lamp on a table in the window and withdraw.

A shot rang out.

The window and lamp shattered simultaneously as Doc threw himself to the ground. The light was extinguished and the safety of darkness restored. Doc got to his feet fast, hoping that nothing more obnoxious than dust had gotten on his worsted wool suit, and crept behind the cover of a pile of empty barrels on the edge of the street. He was not sure from where the shot had been fired—probably from directly across the street—and had only just begun to realize that it had been friendly fire, picking off, as it did, the lamp that illuminated him as an easy target. Presumably it was Raider who had fired the shot.

Doc's eye first of all caught the wavering light and dark shadows inside the shattered window and then the yellow and orange flicker of flames, which grew rapidly and ran like deadly spiders up the drapes and across the inside walls of the shack.

Once again the street outside the building was being lit up, though this time the illumination was softer, more diffuse and mobile, causing the shadows of everything to leap about as if the objects were moving. But nothing moved. Doc had a strong sense of hidden people as he crouched behind the barrels and waited. He could hear the fire now, crackling as it ate up the shack.

The door of the burning house flew open, and a man carrying a rifle burst out and broke for cover. A shot. The man crumpled and dropped his rifle. He sat in the street for a moment, clutching his chest by the light of the flames, and then toppled slowly onto his side. He did not move again.

With a dull roar, the interior of the house collapsed into a fireball as the roof fell in. Doc and a man toting a shotgun, standing not thirty feet away, saw each other at the same instant in the sudden burst of light. Doc ripped off a fast shot at him as he raised the shotgun to his shoulder, and the shotgun discharged into the ground as the man staggered and fell.

Lamps had been lit by now in many of the previously lifeless and darkened shacks. Men rushing down the street to put out the fire slowed when they heard the shots. They advanced more cautiously but still kept coming, in spite of the gunfire, because of the danger of the fire spreading. Fires that started like this frequently leveled the wooden shantytowns of mining communities. Everyone knew their only chance was to catch the flames before they grew too high, or, failing that, to let the fire burn itself out but to contain it by putting out the incendiary sparks that landed on the roofs and walls of nearby buildings. When it came to saving the town, a small thing like gunshots could not be allowed to interfere.

Doc's ambushers, also aware of the approaching townsmen, scattered and ran for it. Doc let them go, but Raider's rifle cracked in rapid fire after them till he had emptied his weapon. Doc saw it spit fire from the roof of a store across the street. There were four or at most five men—little more than darting shadows that showed for a second as they ran behind the houses toward the center of town. Raider hit none of them.

"Come on!" he hissed to Doc. "Let's get the hell outta here too. Unless you want to stick around and explain the blaze."

Doc didn't need any more urging. He heard Raider jump

down from the roof of the store, and together they too ran along behind the houses through the darkness toward the lights of the hotel and the saloons.

CHAPTER FIVE

Raider felt down, in low spirits, the next morning, and he was glad to ride out of town alone at first light. The main street was already busy. Wagons were being loaded with provisions for the outlying mining camps, and men were saddling up their horses and preparing to move out. Raider could still hear the sounds of activity long after the town itself had vanished behind him in the pine trees. Then he heard the black-powder blasts and the hammers of the miners echoing in the valleys all around. Mining fever wakes a man early. Most of them would keep it up with hardly a pause until sundown, and keep at it day after day till they had enough ore dug and milled to load down a train of burros. They'd drive the beasts of burden over the mountains, sell the ore, blow the money in a lot less time than it took them to earn it, and come back into the hills to search and dig once more. At least it beat being a Pinkerton.

No man ever struck it rich being a Pinkerton, that was for sure. And the miners didn't have to write up fool reports and accounts of expenses and find themselves tied by regulations at every turn. A miner didn't have to put up with a slick Easterner in fashionable suits and a derby for a partner either. Raider mused on the drawbacks and disadvantages of his job as he rode into the mountains, now lit in all kinds of pinks and yellows by the sun clearing the horizon. His and the horse's breaths sent plumes into the chill morning mountain air. In spite of himself, Raider was beginning to feel a little better about the world in general.

He came across four miners operating their claim. They had struck water somewhere in the tunnel and were splashing about ankle-deep in the stuff, loading ore into a hopper. The water flowed into a wooden spillway that led to a flotation tank, which separated the ore-bearing rock from the gangue—the ore floating and the heavier useless rock sinking. Even in the early morning chill the four miners were sweating profusely. Raider waved and moved on— being a Pinkerton was not so bad after all.

He rode for another two hours before he began to leave the mining area. He was entering Indian country, on his daily search that now included Ouray and Mr. Hot Stuff as well as Arcady T. Harrison. Today he would traverse an area that for some reason the Utes believed was infested with spirits and which they avoided. It wasn't that he felt he had completely covered the other areas—that would be impossible for him to do, because no matter how thoroughly he searched, those he searched for could easily sidestep him. Raider had to make them come to him somehow, and shouting insults at them was still the only method in which he had any belief.

His complaint was what wandering around all day through valleys, shouting insults, did to his head. Ever since the old Indian told him that the rocks in Ute country had ears, he imagined that indeed the implacable stone faces of the mountains in some weird way actually did hear what he said.

After only a short time, Raider began to get an idea why the Utes thought this part of the mountains was haunted by spirits. The place was full of small steep-walled valleys— almost canyons—which were bare rock, dark and cold, even on a sunny day like this one. The wind moaned and made peculiar sounds in many of these valleys, different in each one—a sighing sound in one gloomy, high-walled place that reminded Raider of a big church, and a series of choking gasps in another as if a human was having difficulty breathing, along with whistles, sobs, and baby cries in other places. Some of these notches in the mountain rock were so spooky, Raider skipped yelling insults in them, took a quick look around, and rode on out, hearing his horse's hooves echo off the dark, threatening cliffs.

He nearly fell off his horse when an enormous Indian spirit rose straight up in the air before him. The horse whinnied and reared in fright at the huge object with great eyes and teeth and Indian warpaint. It came floating through the air directly at Raider, not having to walk on the ground like a mortal being—but wafted along in an ethereal ghostly manner and came in for a direct attack on this white intruder and noisemaker in the holy place of the Ute spirits.

A man like Raider dies fighting, no matter what the odds may be or how overwhelming the enemy. He hauled his Winchester .30–.30 carbine from its saddle sheath, levered a cartridge into the firing chamber, and aimed for the right eye of the creature. As he had expected, the bullet had no effect on this apparition from the other world, but still he emptied the carbine into it, levering and shooting the shells from the hip after his first carefully aimed shot. He dropped the empty carbine and quick-drew his Remington .44 six-gun as the thing was almost upon him. Then he saw an even more amazing thing. The big slugs from his pistol were tearing huge holes in the Indian spirit. It had begun to sag and collapse. The sixth .44 slug brought it to the ground. Raider jumped off his horse, pulled his bowie knife, and went in for the kill.

He stopped, amazed, when two men appeared from beneath the collapsing folds of the monster. In firing at the thing's eyes, he had not seen what he saw now—a wickerwork basket suspended beneath the great globe of the object. One of the men was a big Ute with an eagle feather hanging from his hair. The Indian smiled at Raider and seemed pleased with what he had done. The other was the little miner he and Doc had seen the previous night with Laura Winton. This man was cursing while he quenched a small fire.

It was afternoon by the time Raider located Doc Weatherbee, got him saddled, and brought him out.

"I'd never seen a balloon before," Raider explained. "Hell, I might even have known what it was if it didn't have big eyes and teeth and warpaint on it and if I hadn't half expected some of those Indian spirits to attack me anyway."

Doc raised an eyebrow. "You thought a balloon with two aeronauts was an Indian spirit attacking you, so you shot it down. If I were you, I'd try to put that some other way in my report to Allan Pinkerton."

"I ain't putting it in any goddamn report. I'm the one who found Arcady T. Harrison, not you. That's what you're pissed off about."

"Raider, I'm delighted you've located the missing genius. It saves us spending weeks in a shantytown on top of the world. I was running short of cheroots too, and none of the stores in Mineral Point carries my brand. That's why I got word out right away that you found Harrison. As soon as the horseman reaches a telegraph office, the message will be on its way to Chicago. It's less trouble for us to wait here for the reply than to trek across the mountains and maybe to have to return here again. Hell, Raider, I'm pleased you found Harrison without my help. It's about time you did something yourself without my setting it up for you."

"I knew you'd be green with envy," Raider chuckled, happy that Doc had to concede all the credit to him on this and not about to have his pleasure spoiled by a few acid remarks, no matter how much truth was in them. He had beaten Doc out, fair and square. He wasn't going to let that slick Easterner rub his face into his mistake about that balloon—which could have happened to anyone who had never seen a balloon before.

They made their way across the hills and valleys, pausing sometimes to make sure they were not being followed, although this would have been no easy task for anyone to do without being seen. They maintained these precautions by unspoken mutual agreement until it could be decided between them what course of action to take with Harrison. After identifying Harrison and making sure he would show again by threatening to divulge what he was doing if he disappeared again, Raider's first act was to bring Doc onto the scene. As of now, they were keeping an open mind on how things might go. Raider didn't like to discuss abstract matters in advance, and Doc respected his wishes in this instance since it was Raider's show.

Harrison and Ouray were there when Raider and Doc arrived. Harrison showed more interest in the food and whiskey the Pinkertons had brought with them from town than in discussing his situation. They ate and drank while Doc and Raider examined the tattered remnants of the balloon.

"So this is what he wanted all the brown paper for," Doc said to Raider. "The man is crazy to go up in a balloon made of brown paper."

"I guess with Ouray's weight in the basket," Raider said, "it wasn't going to go too far off the ground anyway."

Harrison overheard them and said, "Absolutely wrong, gentlemen! If you gave me a paper balloon large enough, I could lift a house for you."

"Aren't you supposed to be smelting ore?" Doc asked.

"A tiresome notion, a misapprehension—a rigid conception resulting from a lack of firsthand knowledge of the problems and terrain involved." Harrison dismissed the idea as if it had been Doc's instead of his own.

"From what I understand," Doc said patiently, "the investors who hired us to find you still believe that you are working on a process to smelt pure silver from the ore here in the mountains and then move the silver ingots out by burro instead of the huge volume of ore that goes out presently."

"I once may have believed something like that was feasible," Harrison said in a dismissive way. "No longer. The opportunities for theft on the trek through the mountains would be great. No one would steal ore, but they will steal relatively pure silver. That alone makes the project invalid."

Doc was becoming increasingly annoyed at Harrison's offhand superior attitude, forgetting of course that this was what Raider often accused his partner of also.

"Mr. Harrison, we two Pinkertons were hired just to locate you," Doc told him. "Nothing else. We have already sent a report that you are here, alive and well. What you do or don't do is of no professional concern to us."

Harrison looked at him in alarm. "You've already sent word that you've found me?"

"Yes."

He looked from Doc to Raider. "You boys have really missed out on something big. I would have cut you in for a percentage of the profits if you'd kept your mouths closed."

Raider winked at Doc, as it occurred to them simultaneously how, according to Major Wheeler, Harrison had already sold interests to both the New York financiers and Calvin Thornton.

"Thornton seems mighty eager to find you about some business arrangement you had with him," Raider said. "He's got hired guns hunting all over for you."

Harrison looked a bit uncomfortable. "Does Cal know I'm here?"

"Not yet, he doesn't," Raider said. "But he's been gunning for Doc here because he thinks he's one of your New York backers. Soon as we get back to Mineral Point, we're going to identify ourselves as Pinkertons to all and sundry and tell them we found you, but we don't have to say where."

"It seems kind of dumb to stay out here now that everyone will know you're around," Doc said. "Especially since you could be in town with Laura Winton."

That did it. The investor's eyes shone with anticipation at that name.

"I tried to get Ouray to find me an Indian girl," he said. "But nothing doing."

Ouray looked stern. "We are here to work. What about your work if you go back to live in that town? No. You stay here and make more balloons."

Doc and Raider looked at the Ute chief in surprise. They wondered what his stake in the operation was.

Doc said, "Do you mind if I ask out of personal curiosity why you two are sitting out in this godforsaken place with a brown paper balloon?"

"You must keep this confidential," Harrison cautioned.

"Our work is done," Doc said. "Our job was to find you, not find out what you're doing. We won't say a word about that—either in our reports or to anyone we meet. Unless of course we get orders from headquarters to find out."

Harrison grinned. When he did this, his mouth twisted off to one side, giving his head an irregular appearance. As he began to explain his project to them, he changed from being a cantankerous, egotistical individual into an almost youthful enthusiast in spite of his fifty-plus years.

"Balloons, gentlemen, balloons! That's how I'm going to take the ore out. By low-cost disposable paper balloons which will cost practically nothing to make, can be brought in by the thousand folded up into the size of a large book, and which need only a small oil heater to fill them with hot air. It's the concept of the century! A great leap forward for mankind!"

Doc sat on a rock and lit an Old Virginian cheroot. He could think of several reasons why the inventor had not communicated this concept yet to the New York financiers backing him, the chief one being they would think him crazy and withdraw their funding. However, he could see that Arcady T. was troubled by no such doubts.

"You talk about the railroad," Arcady said to Doc, although Doc hadn't said a word about railroads. "You think that's the greatest marvel on earth—a locomotive using steam from boiling water to pull great loads from the Atlantic to the Pacific. I tell you that's just a primitive beginning. Why build bridges, why lay rails, why manufacture engines, when all the power man ever needs is literally in front of his nose? Of course he doesn't notice it till it blows his hat off. That's right, gentlemen. You have arrived in this part of Colorado at a great historic moment—the harnessing of air power for commercial transportation. This will be something to relate to your grandchildren. People will come to hear you lecture on how you met me on a lonely mountain in the Colorado wilderness, accompanied only by a Ute Indian, as I envisioned and planned the airborne cargo system that revolutionized the world. Alas, I will be long gone by then, expired from my labors, fled to join other immortal names in the hallowed halls of—"

"I thought the Montgolfier brothers invented balloons," Doc interrupted in a flat voice.

"Good heavens, yes," Arcady acknowledged, coming back to earth again. "I have no claim on that. Ah, the Montgolfier brothers, my heroes, I would not steal credit from them. Joseph was the dreamer, it was all his idea, and Etienne was the practical man of the world. They launched their first balloon unmanned, on June 4, 1783—almost a century ago! It had a diameter of thirty-five feet and was constructed of four segments fastened together with eighteen hundred buttons. The material was sackcloth lined with three layers of paper, and they lit a fire of wool and straw in a brazier beneath it to heat the air. The flight lasted about ten minutes, and after the balloon landed, it burst into flames."

Harrison stood and pulled a rolled sheet of paper from his bag. It was a hand-colored engraving of a balloon with a pattern of gold decorations on a blue background.

Raider laughed. "It looks like wallpaper."

"Exactly," Harrison said. "They made this one from two layers of wallpaper with a layer of taffeta between. Unfortunately it rained the day of its launching and the entire balloon fell into pieces."

Ouray spoke. "Tell them about the balloon before that one."

"I don't know why that one interests you so much, Ouray. It was the first flight with hydrogen gas inside the balloon. The balloon was only twelve feet in diameter, because in those days collecting the inflammable hydrogen gas was very dangerous. This unmanned balloon disappeared into the clouds, which were at about fifteen hundred feet, and continued its ascent until it burst. Having taken off in Paris, it came down nearly an hour later twelve miles to the north. When it dropped out of the sky into a field, the peasants attacked it with pitchforks and dragged what they thought was its great carcass into the village of Gonesse."

Ouray doubled up with laughter at this.

"The first air voyage in America took place on January 9, 1793, in Philadelphia," Arcady resumed. "So you see I claim no credit for inventing balloons. My name will go down in history as the first man to put them into regular commercial use. Though I should add that when Benjamin Franklin witnessed the first manned balloon flight in Paris and was asked what use such a thing had, he replied, 'What use is a newborn baby?'"

"I grant you that moving ore out of the San Juan by balloon would greatly improve matters around here," Doc said. "But what of the practical difficulties? How could you steer them? What's to stop the balloon from just rising up till it bursts?"

Harrison was really excited now, waving his arms and talking in increasingly rapid streams. "No trouble there. None at all. Forget the mountains for a moment and visualize this area as a flat plain. The prevailing wind is from west to east, and so is favorable to us most of the time. The climate is dry, and when precipitation occurs it will often be as snow, which will not damage the paper as much as rain would. The load carried by the balloon controls the height at which it flies, and therefore it should be easy to settle on a regulation-size balloon that carries a particular weight of ore at a particular height, say thirty feet above ground level. Do you know what a trail rope is? Balloons use them all the time. Generally they are let down shortly after takeoff. The trail rope is a stout rope attached to the hoop to which the cording of the balloon is also tied. It trails along the ground behind the balloon and acts as a restraining balance. The more rope let out, the lighter the load, and so the balloon rises. However, as the balloon rises, it has to lift a greater weight of rope off the ground and thus its ascent is checked. The rope can control the balloon's altitude almost indefinitely in a light steady wind, and you can easily imagine a whole caravan of balloons tethered loosely together, all trailing their ropes, making their way at twenty-five miles per hour—that's an average—across a plain and gently bearing great loads of silver ore for the distant smelters. It would work if it weren't for one thing."

Doc nodded. "Mountains."

Harrison was off again. "But I can beat them. You see,

mountains would be no problem at all if I were considering manned balloons, since the crew could raise or lower the trail rope as required and adjust the heater. But the whole basis of my project is to standardize everything so that nothing need be adjusted during the journey from the mines to the smelter. For this I must find a suitable route out of here directly to the east. I went out myself by Slumgullion Pass, across the Cebolla, and down Spring Gulch to the valley of the Rio Grande. I followed the Rio Grande as it zigzagged east as far as Del Norte, and then I cut across country to the San Luis Lakes and the Great San Dunes. I crossed the mountains there by Mosca Pass and finished up south of Pueblo, not far north of Walsenburg. A smelter could be built anywhere there, with access to the railroad north to Denver. The distance east from here to there as the crow flies, which is the way balloons travel, is only about a hundred and fifty miles—instead of twice that by burro. And when you compare the speed of a balloon in a favorable wind with that of a burro on a mountain trail, the comparison's laughable. At twenty-five miles per hour, one of my balloons could complete the journey in six hours! Unbelievable, especially when compared with the weeks it takes a loaded-down burro!"

In spite of himself, Doc felt fired up by Arcady's project. "You think you can make it work?"

"Of course I can make it work!" Arcady waved his arms. "I can't bring in silk or hydrogen for the most advanced sort of balloons, but these cheap paper constructions can afford to be lost with their loads in some quantity and still pay off because of their much greater efficiency and speed. I foresee a nonstop procession of them from west to east during the daylight hours, following a well-established route and guided by men on the ground at outposts along the way."

Raider had lost interest in the details of the plan and wanted to hear what it was like to fly a balloon. "How high up can you go?" he asked.

"So high there is hardly any air to breathe—a bit like when you first come up into the mountains from the plain; you feel light-headed and short of breath, but much more so. I'll take you up, if you like."

"Not in a paper balloon above an oil fire," Raider said decisively.

Harrison laughed. "I try not to think of that myself. Only last year something happened to the balloon of a friend of mine while it was aloft. He was thought to have been at an elevation of about three miles when it happened. Assuming that to be the distance he fell, since he weighed about a hundred and sixty pounds, he hit the earth with a momentum equal to 160,800 pounds, or a little more than eighty tons—that's with a mean velocity of 495 feet per second. Either he was scattered in tiny pieces or was buried deep in the earth. They recovered the balloon, but they never found him."

Doc and Raider exchanged a glance. There was something weird about the way Harrison could cheerfully relate his precise calculations of the factors involved in his friend's fatal misfortune.

"I can't imagine what it must be like, moving around up there, looking down," Raider said.

"It's not so strange during a daytime flight," Arcady told him. "You can identify all sorts of familiar things below you and see landscape you know well in interesting new ways. But at nighttime, especially alone on a cloudless night without much wind, it's very different. Up there alone beneath the stars, you feel you are the only person really awake and alive, only you are aware of what is happening at this moment, and often you suddenly feel frightened and so lonely you wish you had not made the ascent. At nighttime the earth is deathly quiet. You can't see anything, but you can hear things. On a still night at twenty-five hundred feet I have heard cicadas in the trees beneath. At three thousand feet over a lake I heard bullfrogs croaking. At five thousand feet I've heard shouts and the crowing of a cock. At six thousand the bark of a dog and report of a gun. And at ten thousand feet the whistle of a train. These sounds only make you feel more isolated and alone up there in the darkness."

Raider's mouth hung open in amazement at this information. He looked in awe at Harrison's animated little figure, seeing him as a man of courage for the first time. Then he looked a little shamefacedly at the tattered remains of the balloon he had shot down.

"Sorry about that," Raider said.

The young miner's mind was not on his job. While he shoveled ore into the handmade wooden ore car on the narrow tracks he had laid himself, he thought about his girl back in Kansas. He hadn't seen her in two years now, and sometimes these days, now that it would soon come time to go back and fetch her, he would wake from a nightmare in which he had gone back to her father's ranch only to find she had not waited for him like she promised she would. When he had that dream, he would wake in a panic and it would be a full minute or more as he sat up in his bedding, alone in his mountainside shack in the San Juan, before he realized where he was, that it was only a dream, a bad dream. The nightmare of learning she had not waited for him was more than he could take—what would he do then? All this work—everything he had suffered and labored for over the past two years—would be for nothing. He didn't give a damn for money. It was what the money would allow him to do with her that counted.

He would go back with enough money to buy a spread of his own. They would marry in Kansas and leave right away for Oregon. Kansas was spoken for, but he had heard of the new land being opened up in the Northwest and that today there was opportunity out there like there had been in Kansas twenty years ago. Nothing could stop him succeeding in Oregon. He had proved himself here in the San Juan.

He was getting more than $100 of silver per ton of milled ore and stashing his money in a bank in Pueblo. He didn't drink, whore, or gamble. He only thought about his girl back in Kansas and put his profits in the bank for them both. Neither of them could read or write, so all he had to go on was her promise to him before he left and his belief in her that she would be true to him, that she would wait for him. Yet he often told himself that she had no way of knowing even if he was still alive, let alone whether he had forgotten her. This fall when the snows came he would collect his savings and go back for her. It was time. No more waiting.

When the ore car was filled, he pushed it on the rails alongside the wooden spillway he had built to channel the water to power his mill. The hard labor and his daydreams of the girl he had left behind in Kansas, together with his solitude day after day on this mountainside, had made him unobservant of the world around him—all his eyes saw was the grade of the ore and the future it would buy him.

He never saw the Ute who watched him on horseback from among the trunks of the pines on the slope. He didn't see the Indian dismount, tie his horse to a branch, and slowly approach.

The Ute was tall, strong, and supple. One side of his face and the front of his neck, continuing under his buckskin tunic, was scarred into knots, curls, and twists like the skin of a rough-barked tree. Those familiar with the scars of fire victims would have recognized the terrible burn marks and wonder how flames had done this. Few this far west would ever have seen the ravages of a chemical burn, worse by far than one received from the flames of timber combustion.

The eyes were untouched, as was the great hooked nose. The long black hair served to cover much of the disfigurement, except for the mouth. On the side of the face that was burned, half of the upper lip was gone, revealing the long white upper teeth to their gums and roots. Mr. Hot Stuff moved like a shadow from tree to tree.

When he came out into the open, he was no more than twenty feet from the miner. The miner continued at his work, unaware of Mr. Hot Stuff walking slowly toward him. He was only eight feet away when the miner suddenly looked up and saw him. Mr. Hot Stuff saw first the look of surprise and fear on the miner's face, then the unarmed man's involuntary glance to where he had left a rifle propped against a tree trunk, and finally the look of revulsion as the man's eyes strayed to the disfigurement—quickly replaced by a stiff smile.

"Hello," the miner said, as if he were pleased to see his visitor.

Mr. Hot Stuff drew his revolver.

"There's no need for that," the young miner said. "Do you understand English? What do you want?"

Mr. Hot Stuff said nothing. He squeezed the trigger once and a bullet smashed into the chest cavity of the miner. The man fell on his back. The Ute holstered the pistol and stooped over his victim, who was muttering something.

It might be weeks before they would find the body here, Mr. Hot Stuff reasoned. He would have to leave a sign. Another white man killed by Indians would be sure to cause major trouble. Certainly it would flush out Ouray, wherever he was hiding, so that he could prevent the Army from coming in. Mr. Hot Stuff was almost sure Ouray was alive, because his wife and family were not mourning him. Ouray must have sent them a sign. When Ouray showed, Mr. Hot

Stuff would ambush him—or cause the Army to come in so that Ouray would have to fight them and die. Without Ouray, Mr. Hot Stuff could come back and live as he had a right to on the land of his ancestors. No one would dare stand against him. Except Ouray. And he knew he could not kill Ouray by himself.

He drew his knife and knelt beside the dying miner, who was still saying something.

As Mr. Hot Stuff cut across the man's forehead below the hairline and separated the scalp from the bone of the skull beneath, the miner's eyes opened and he spoke distinctly.

"I'm gonna marry her and go directly to Oregon. She's waiting for me now back in Kansas."

CHAPTER SIX

Cigar smoke filled the room. Calvin Thornton had almost to peer through it at three of his men. "I expected you hours ago," he said.

"We had to stop on the trail, boss, and help some people. There was a blond scalp hanging from a stick by a rawhide thong on the side of the trail where a path led away. Some men were already there, wanting to go down and see what was there, but they was afraid of being bushwhacked. So we went along with them."

Thornton's face grew grim. "Another miner?"

"A young fella," the second man put in. "I never seed him afore in town."

The first man resumed his narrative. "He was dead only a few hours, I reckon. So we brought his body into town and left it at the marshal's office."

Thornton nodded his approval. "Everything all right at the smelter?"

"One bit of trouble—which I took care of," the first man volunteered. "This loudmouth was down from Denver saying you and some other assayers are cheating the miners here. He said that although you give the miners a honest count on the silver content of their ore, you don't pay them a cent for the gold you also find in the ore. He claimed this gold content is sometimes worth more than the silver content of the ore, and he said that the miners are so happy because you're paying $1.29 for silver, they don't bother with the gold. Which is what's making the likes of you a fortune."

"And?" Thornton's voice was tight.

"I shot him and put him in the river."

"Right place for him," Thornton agreed. "What else?"

"Nothing much. Things is running smooth."

Thornton looked at the two other men. "Same with you?" They nodded.

"Leave well enough alone then and stay here in Mineral Point," Thornton went on, "because I think you're going to be needed. That scalped miner you saw is just one of the things happening here. Wheeler, the Indian agent, thinks it's an outcast who's doing the killing, but you can never tell with those Utes. He was supposed to have killed Chief Ouray, too—but then Ouray reappears, with that little rat Harrison, who was gone too. This is according to two Pinkertons."

"Pinkertons?"

"The quack we tried to kill that night down by the hardware store turned out to be a Pinkerton. The second Pinkerton is the fella I hired to spy on the first one."

"Raider?" one man asked, amazed.

Thornton nodded and spat in the cuspidor. "That bastard has killed three of my men so far, as well as taking me for forty dollars."

"What are you going to do about him, boss?"

Thornton held up a hand in alarm. "Nothing! And leave the quack alone too! I count myself lucky that none of you were good enough to bushwhack either of them that night. Last thing I need is a whole swarm of those nosy bastard Pinkertons sniffing around here because one of their pals was cut down by you lot. Be careful about how you boys handle the Utes as well. Lot of people in town feel we're sitting on a keg of gunpowder with them. If some damn thing makes them Injuns real mad, it might be years before they quiet down again. We don't want to lose the San Juan because of some stupid incident. I know I can trust you three, and I'm depending on you to ride herd on the others— especially the ones who are half loco. They answer to you, and you answer to me. If they can't understand that, pay them off and give them a bit extra to clear town. I don't need no loose cannons around."

The men nodded.

"You said Harrison showed up with Chief Ouray?" one man asked.

"Yeah. He's been hiding out in the Ute country. It seems the Pinkertons were hired to find him by the New York financiers. My guess is that some of these financiers will show up in town real soon to see what the hell Harrison is up to now that they know he's alive. Whatever Harrison does or does not do, I am not going to allow Wall Street manipulators to steal my business from me. We couldn't find Harrison. They did. We don't know what Harrison is doing. Let their money pay to find out. Whatever Harrison develops, I'll own it, so long as these financiers don't get a foothold in this town."

One of the men said, "These here finance men are slippery types, boss, so I've been told."

"You've been told right. They got their agents and their lawyers and politicians to back them up. They got nine and ten of everything, more than they ever need. But there's one thing every Wall Street financier owns only one of, and that's his life. If he knows he's going to lose that by setting foot in the San Juan, nary a one of them will come this side of the Mississippi—after we make an example of the first one."

Like every western mining town, Mineral Point was a moody place. Sometimes for weeks on end the streets and saloons would be almost as quiet as any orderly town back east, and the miners would work solemnly and grimly at their laborious tasks without ever seeming to need to let off a head of steam. Then one day, for no particular reason, triggered by no particular incident or individual, all hell would break loose. It might be high spirits with no harm done, or it might be a murderous brawl that left the dust on the street caked with congealed blood and added another couple of timber crosses in the graveyard on the hill outside town. Usually it was a mixture of both good-fellowship and homicidal differences.

It so happened that Mineral Point was going through one of its manic phases while Raider and Doc were there. Even in mid-afternoon, with the sun beating down on the dusty street, folks were living it up like they normally did only after dark. The tables were filled with cardplayers in all the gambling houses, the girls were working round the clock with almost no rest in the bordellos, and barmen could hardly keep the glasses filled in the saloons. Working stiffs loading goods into wagons had to put up with throngs of drunks who found them funny. Everyone had to duck when some celebrating miner tried to shoot his six-gun in the air cowboy-style, because the miner's calloused, work-hardened hand was not accustomed to fingering a pistol, and he was as liable to shoot himself in the foot or someone else in the head as he was to twirl a quick-drawn gun by its trigger guard and then shoot it high and safe in the air.

Few of the fights pitted miner against miner. Mostly it was miner versus townie—usually a gambler or drifter the miner had decided was taking advantage of him. And it wasn't always the miners who lost the fight. The miner's opponent might be faster or more adroit, but often he lacked the miner's ferocity. It took a certain kind of belief in oneself to dig and scratch for silver in the side of a mountain in the wilderness, and such a man, through sheer forcefulness, can overcome a more skilled opponent in a barroom or street brawl. When the miners did fight each other, it was usually only with their fists. Those fighting each other one minute would buy drinks for each other the next—after they had picked themselves up and could not rightly remember what they had been quarreling about.

Raider was in his element. He and Doc knew that the only rest they ever got as Pinkertons was when they were beyond the reach of the Chicago office. Like soldiers in a long war, they knew how to enjoy any respite in the hostilities without asking too many questions. However, it was during such times that personality differences and mutual irritation surfaced most strongly between the two men. United as partners against a common enemy, they functioned as a team. Left to their own devices, they had the time to consider each other's faults.

"No sign of a telegram from Chicago?" Raider would ask at least once a day, because in a way he was like a guilty schoolboy playing hooky. He vaguely felt it was wrong for him not to be out there working.

"Raider, it has to come in by horse," Doc told him every time. "It'll be a few days yet. My guess is they'll order us to stay on here to keep an eye on Harrison, now that we've found him, until they send someone here themselves to talk with him."

Raider looked across the crowded hotel saloon to a table at which Arcady T. Harrison and Laura Winton sat, drinking and laughing. "The little twit doesn't look so bad now he's cleaned himself up."

Harrison's appearance had changed totally from the time he had moved about incognito as a scruffy miner. Yet he had not returned to an eastern mode of dress. He had decked himself out like a gambler in a sharp black suit, brightly colored vest, and ruffled silk shirt with a string necktie. Had he been a foot taller, he would have been a striking figure—had he also been handsome, which he was not.

However out of place he looked in this garb, he seemed very pleased with himself. Much of his happiness had to do with the fact that he was back enjoying the benefits of a town life, simple as they were, after his stay on the mountainside with only Ouray for company. Laura Winton was certainly an improvement over that.

She hung on the little inventor's every word, looked adoringly in his face, and behaved almost like a lady in his company. He seemed to have forgotten all about balloons and revolutionizing the mining of the San Juan for the pleasures to be found in Laura's bed and the saloons of Mineral Point.

"I seen Calvin Thornton talking to Arcady early today," Raider said. "He gave him money."

Doc raised an eyebrow. "I guess Thornton bought himself some paper balloons. I bet he'll kick Harrison's ass and make him produce. Anyway, it's none of our business."

"That's the way I see it," Raider agreed.

"Unless Harrison is threatened."

Raider glanced across again at the little man, who was waving his arms and apparently singing or reciting something. "He sure don't look too threatened right now."

"Thornton won't wait forever."

Raider looked around the bar. The number of his acquaintances had dropped sharply when word got out he was a Pinkerton, but those who stayed friendly more than made up for those who stayed away. He saw a few miners he knew standing at the bar and was about to join them when he spotted a woman sitting alone at a table. She was pretty in a demure way, in a modest dress with a high collar that hid a lot more than it revealed. Doc's eyes followed the direction of Raider's stare. Raider got to his feet right away, knowing that if he gave Doc a chance, he would never get this lady for himself. If she was available. He had only one way of finding that out—by asking if he could join her.

"See you some other time," he muttered at Doc, picked his hat off the table, and headed across the saloon to the lady solo at her table. Doc watched him go.

Then came the part that Raider dreaded. What if she screamed when he asked if he could join her at the table? Or shouted at him to go away? He would have to swagger away to the bar like he couldn't have cared less. He was already rehearsing his retreat before he spoke a word to her.

"Hello, ma'am. Mind if I join you?"

He hadn't meant it to sound so sharp and rasping—he knew his tone was more fitting for a cardplayer asking to join a poker game than for a stranger approaching a pretty woman in a public place.

To his surprise, she waved to an empty chair beside her.

In his clumsiness in getting into the chair, he shook the table and spilled her drink. At least it gave him something to talk about and made her smile.

"It was gin," she informed him.

He ordered for them and soon stopped feeling awkward as she chatted with him and seemingly quite naturally never lapsed into awkward silences as they would have done had the conversational lead been left to him. Raider was so grateful for her easy ways, he even lightened up on his whiskey consumption. Hell, he was willing to make a sacrifice for a pretty woman.

And pretty she was. Unlike most of the other women who frequented the saloons, she played down her beauty rather than exaggerate it. Apart from her modest costume, her face was unpainted, and her hair was pulled back severely. She had calm hazel eyes, a small mouth set in a permanently wistful expression, and freckles on her upturned nose. She couldn't be more than twenty-two, Raider decided, and was most definitely a full-fledged woman and quite assured in his company.

Raider noticed a couple of miners sit at Doc's table and

knew from their glances they were talking about the woman he was with. Doc looked across at her several times with lingering curiosity, and Raider was afraid that he might come over and join them and try to steal this woman from him. He once caught Doc's eye and received one of his sardonic smiles. Raider wondered for a moment why all this looking and talking were going on, and decided they were jealous of him. From that point on, he devoted his full attention to the lady in his company. Her name was Alice.

The afternoon sun was getting low in the sky when Raider decided to ask her to come with him to his hotel room. If Doc could get women to go to bed with him this early in the day, so could he. He only wished now he had gotten himself a better hotel room.

"If you don't mind," Alice said, "since I live here in town and it would cause talk if I went to the hotel room with you, why don't you come home with me instead?"

She had accepted!

"Right now?" Raider asked, letting his anticipation show.

She smiled. "If you like."

Raider hustled her out of the place and cast a triumphant look back at Doc as he went out the door. Doc still had that annoyingly superior smile on his face.

She lived in a freshly painted two-room cabin that was well furnished and clean. Raider wondered for the first time who she was and what she did for a living, but felt he could hardly ask her now. She didn't seem to be a sporting woman, and yet how could he be sure? He vaguely acknowledged to himself that she must have a good income to live in a comfortable house like this.

"Do you like my little home, Raider?" Alice asked coyly, leading him from the front to the back room.

"Sure, yeah, it's great."

Raider watched her go to the double bed, turn down the

spread, and fluff the pillows. She looked at him invitingly. He walked toward her. . . .

At that moment the street door was unlocked and thrown open. At the sound of heavy boots crossing the floor of the front room, Raider's hand strayed to his holstered gun.

A thin, haggard man in his fifties rushed into the back room. Raider recognized him as a local storekeeper. He was unarmed.

"That's my wife!" he shouted at Raider and needlessly pointed at Alice.

"It is?"

"The slut brings men here to torment me, making sure to walk them past my store on the way. One of these days I'll stay put and let her give her body to some stranger."

"Oh, no, Harry," Alice cried, running to her husband. "Never let me do that!"

They embraced.

Raider shook his head in disbelief and headed for the street.

On his way to the stables to ride out of town awhile, he thought about seeking Doc out to tell him about this pair. Then it occurred to him that Doc already knew about Alice's tricks—that this was what the miners had been telling him as they sat at Doc's table and looked across at Raider and her. None of them had done a thing to warn him, of course. He could still see that sarcastic smile on Doc's face.

The passengers had to climb out of the open wagon for the steeper descents, as they had done for the ascents on the other side of the pass.

"It would have been easier to walk all the way to Mineral Point in the first place," a lady passenger declared in an aggrieved tone, "in place of all this climbing in and out of this infernal wagon."

Yet when they saw the slopes the wagon had to travel

up or down, they made haste to abandon it, trusting more to their own two feet rather than risk hurtling downward or slipping backward with the big wagon and mule team. The trail was too primitive for anything resembling a stagecoach to travel on it. Those who did not travel light and by horseback or who were unused to tying their possessions to the back of a burro had to load their trunks, hatboxes, and other goods into the open wagon, then climb up after them and make themselves as comfortable as possible on hard wooden benches in what one lady referred to as "exceedingly mixed company."

The drivers of these wagons collected their fares before starting out, and once they had the money pocketed, they tended to put the further welfare of their passengers out of mind. A passenger hit by a falling stone or overhead branch or a bag lost down a ravine as the wagon lurched over a bump were occurrences of little interest to them. Indeed the passengers themselves, after many hours on the trail, became so dispirited they hardly seemed to care what happened to them.

They camped out at night and ate wild game shot by the driver and drank strong coffee made with the water of mountain streams. The ladies shared a tent of canvas stretched from the wagon to two nearby trees, with hanging walls to give them privacy. Gents slept under the stars.

When they had a plentiful supply of customers, the drivers liked to squeeze them aboard twelve to a wagon to make maximum money for their run. When they could, they would pick and choose what passengers they would take, trying to leave behind for other drivers those they recognized as potential problems. Certain of the drivers were raconteurs who liked, after a journey, to entertain their friends in saloons with stories of a 300-mile trek with a nervous female passenger who had to relieve the pressure on her bladder every quarter mile, of an eastern greenhorn armed to the teeth who saw hostile Indians, holdup men, grizzlies, or wolf packs behind every other rock and loosed off so many shots at his imaginary attackers during the ride that everyone at journey's end was either deaf or still tremulously awaiting a sudden gunshot without reason or warning.

Oregon Bill Cassidy, the driver of this particular wagon, was more outgoing with his passengers than some of the other drivers, who grew dour and silent along the trail.

"Keep it going, ladies," he encouraged them as they climbed aboard after a sharp descent, "and we'll be in Mineral Point this evening. That's right, sir, I wouldn't lie to you. We'll do it afore sundown if God wills it and you wonderful people keep on being brave in the face of adversity." He made no attempt to hide his snicker as he paid them this undeserved compliment. This particular bunch had been obnoxious. Now, as they became hysterical with fatigue as well, he held out the reward he had been denying them until this time—a visible end to their sufferings. "Mineral Point's on the other side of that ridge ahead. We go around the ridge along the course of a stream. You've come this far! You're almost there!"

The passengers looked at Oregon Bill so gratefully, one might suppose he had just saved them from some terrible disaster. But he wasn't fooled by their new feelings of goodwill toward him. As soon as he hit town and they felt the security of civilization, such as it was, they would turn on him and treacherously complain about the condition of their baggage and themselves and his treatment of them.

Some had already said loudly they would prefer to put up with a surly, unfriendly driver than be treated to the kind of friendliness Oregon Bill offered his passengers. They were chiefly referring to his excellent memory of every disaster that had taken place along the trail, which he would describe to them in grisly detail before they arrived at the site of its occurrence, so that they had enough time to worry whether the same thing was going to happen to them.

Oregon Bill was chiefly impressed by his lady passengers and scarcely noticed the men unless they were abusing or threatening him. On this journey into Mineral Point, he had found his most interesting passengers to be a mother with her daughter of perhaps sixteen years. The mother constantly warned the daughter to wear her sunbonnet and long mitts in order to protect her complexion, hair, and hands from the sun, and would point out to her as a warning a suntanned farm lass also traveling on the wagon.

"If you don't cover yourself, you'll end up looking like her," the mother admonished, and the daughter, after a quick look at the farm girl, hurriedly covered up her white skin from the sun's rays.

The mother's chief interest was the trailside graves, which were numerous. She questioned Oregon Bill closely on their occupants. He described the ends of those he knew about, and used his imagination on those he didn't.

This pair served to pass his time with their conversation, but Bill was most intrigued by a statuesque beauty who he figured was a music hall singer or something of that kind. She was temperamental, but not in ways Bill would have expected, so he put up with her tantrums. She never complained of climbing in her dainty shoes over the rocky trail like all the other women did, and spent little time adjusting and protecting her clothes—although she was always elegantly and fashionably dressed, so far as Oregon Bill was a judge. She ate the food without complaint, laughed at his jokes, listened to his stories—and then adamantly refused to camp in a particular place because she did not like the view! At another point she insisted that the singing of wild birds was getting on her nerves and banged on an empty bucket with a stick in order to quiet them. She halted the wagon with a loud shriek at the base of a cliff in order to insist that the citified gent with her climb a good way up this cliff to pick a scarlet and white flower growing from a crack in the rock. The poor bastard looked as much in fear of the climb as he was of her to dare refuse to risk his neck in the attempt. When Oregon Bill saw that the man in all probability would fall and break a limb—and have to be cared for in a slowly moving wagon for the rest of the way— Oregon Bill scampered up the rock face past him, plucked the flower, and handed it to him on the way down to present to the lady. She bestowed a smile on Bill and behaved herself for the rest of that day.

Now she was openly skeptical of his latest story of horror and tragedy.

"Madame Avellana," he said, for that was what she called herself, referring to her male companion only as "the baron," much to the amusement of the other passengers, who seemed to have some doubts about his claims of nobility. "As sure as my name is Oregon Bill Cassidy, what I'm telling you is true. This is no tale of bygone terror and horrors of yesteryear." He pointed dramatically into the trailside forest. "He's out there right now, with his face all burned and twisted, with his guns and his big knife that he uses for scalping. . . ."

All twelve passengers looked fearfully among the trunks of the trees as if this apparition might appear at any moment.

One of the men spoke. "He's right, you know. I saw something about these scalpings last week in the *Sagauche Chronicle*. I hadn't realized that this was where they took place."

"T'was right there, where you see that path leading down off the trail, where they found a fair-haired scalp only t'other day. A driver on his way out told me this morning. The victim was a young man from Kansas with a silver mine about a mile down that path you see in front of your eyes."

"Was he handsome?" the sixteen-year-old girl asked.

"That's what I heard, missy," Oregon Bill told her.

"Why are we stopped here?" her mother inquired in a sudden panic. "Whip those mules and let's move along out of this dangerous place."

"Come, driver, hurry on," a male voice called from the back of the wagon. "I have to get to town."

Oregon Bill paused dramatically and bestowed a sinister smile upon them. "It's no use running away. We could never escape from him in this heavy wagon. If Mr. Hot Stuff wants to kill us now, we'll have to stand and fight as best we can. We could never outrun him."

He enjoyed for a moment the deadly silence he had created among his passengers, then in his most easygoing way he turned in his seat and said, "Giddyap" to the team of mules, and the wagon trundled slowly forward.

Oregon Bill was probably the only one who was truly surprised when, only a short distance along the trail, they were confronted by a Ute horseman. They turned a corner in the trail and he was waiting there, sitting bareback on a mustang, a rifle in one arm. They saw now that only one half of his face was disfigured, but even so not a single one of them had any doubt about this man's identity.

Oregon Bill roared at the mules, slapped the reins on their backs, and gave the two lead animals a taste of the whip. The team and wagon lurched forward and came straight at the mounted Indian about thirty yards away.

In one fast movement, the Ute raised his rifle to his shoulder, squeezed off a shot and levered another cartridge into the chamber.

The bullet hit Oregon Bill in the chest. With a loud wheeze, he loosened his grip on the reins, the whip fell from his hand, and he tumbled headfirst between the mules and the wagon, which passed over his body without touching him and left him writhing on the trail behind.

Mr. Hot Stuff did not move out of the way of the galloping mules but let them come to him and slow of their own accord as his mustang ran with them. While he slowed the mules to a stop, he kept a loose cover on the passengers in the wagon with his rifle. The wagon's jolting would have prevented accurate use of weapons by any of its passengers had they drawn them, and they had not.

With the mules now stopped and panting, Mr. Hot Stuff rode warily around to examine the occupants of the wagon. He pulled up his horse and stared at them for a while, as they wondered whether he was doing this simply to frighten them before robbing them and letting them go or whether he was trying to decide which of several terrible things he would do to them. They all sat very quiet and did not look him in his fierce dark eyes. They politely avoided staring at the burned side of his face, except for morbid glances they could not help.

"Mr. Hot Stuff is an asshole!"

They all heard the words distinctly. The gruff male voice came from a gulch to the right of the trail, but it was hard to pinpoint its exact location because of the echoes.

"Miss Hot Stuff dyes her hair!"

Now it was the turn of the Ute warrior to avoid the passengers' gaze. He pulled his horse to the side of the trail and looked down over a drop of seventy feet or so.

"Hot Stuff is coyote shit!"

The Indian glanced back at the people sitting in the wagon as if admitting he had no right to harm them if he could not even stop insults such as this from being shouted at him.

Madame Avellana nudged the baron. "He's not watching. Shoot him."

"I might miss, and then he'll kill the lot of us."

"Give me the gun. I'll do it."

The baron shook his head and moved away from her as much as he could on the crowded bench.

"Mr. Hot Stuff is afraid of Ouray!"

The voice was as loud and clear as before, yet seemed to get neither nearer nor more distant.

Mr. Hot Stuff looked very carefully all about him and without warning urged his mustang into a gallop back along the trail in the direction from which they had come.

They heard no more from the mysterious voice in the gulch. When they walked back to see how Oregon Bill was, they found him dead. The dome of his skull was a glistening bright pink where the skin and hair had been peeled off.

CHAPTER SEVEN

Major Wheeler drummed his fingers on his desk and gazed steadily at Ouray. The ex-Army man had reduced many a tough fighting man to a state of nerves with this treatment. It seemed to have no effect whatsoever on the Ute chief, who sat in the office with as much indifference as if the major had been a woodpecker rapping on a tree.

"This makes four white men shot and scalped," the major summed up for the third time. "It just can't keep happening, Ouray."

The Ute did not react.

"If it hadn't been for that Pinkerton agent Raider shouting insults about him," the major continued, "Mr. Hot Stuff would doubtless have killed everyone aboard that wagon. Raider happened by accidentally and saw nothing. He didn't even realize he had saved their lives till after he got back to Mineral Point. You have to kill Mr. Hot Stuff quickly, Ouray, before he does something worse than he has up till now."

"He won't fight me," Ouray said shortly.

"Then get your warriors together and hunt him down."

The chief looked at the agent in disgust. "That is not the Ute way of doing it."

The major raised his eyes to heaven. "Just consider this, Ouray. What if Mr. Hot Stuff had killed all twelve persons aboard that wagon as well as the driver? Thirteen white people—women as well as men—murdered in Southern Ute country in a single afternoon. Do you think I could keep the Army away after that? I could not. Don't you see that's what Mr. Hot Stuff is trying to do?"

"If the Army comes," Ouray announced, "Mr. Hot Stuff and I will fight side by side against the soldiers."

Wheeler could easily visualize that this indeed might happen, although he could not for the life of him see why Ouray would not "come around," as he put it, and see things in his commonsense way.

"I have come for the money not paid to me while I was away," Ouray said in his usual solemn tones.

This came as a bit of a disappointment to the major, who was hoping to spend this sum on what he regarded as projects beneficial to the Ute people rather than have Ouray disperse it in the form of alcohol.

"Why should you receive government money as the chief of the Souther Ute people if you are away from your job?" the major demanded.

"Job?" Ouray asked, puzzled. "I have come for the money because I am chief."

Wheeler cut a long, pointless conversation short by promising to give him the money.

"Yet when I pay you this money as great chief," the major added, "I have to wonder if that is what you still are. Does Mr. Hot Stuff think of you as a great chief?"

"He will." Ouray sounded definite.

Imelda Avellana arrived in Mineral Point with the fuss and bother she felt was her due, except that it was not on her account. She had been upstaged by this Indian and the death of their wagon driver. However, she could readily see that these were events beyond management's control, and she graciously decided that she would enter the town, as she put it to the manager of the Hotel San Juan on the entrance steps, "in all humility, out of respect for the memory of their heroic driver." She repeated this twice for the benefit of the *Mineral Point Gazette* reporter, who happened to be present too.

"I will also sing an aria in his memory," she added, "at my opening performance tonight. You might mention that I will be appearing four times nightly for the next three weeks."

The hotel's new manager, whose idea it was to employ her, was suitably impressed by her appearance. Madame Avellana was in her early thirties and was a trifle buxom, but this was countered by her quick, graceful movements and sharp features. She had the classical Greek look that sculptors of monuments like to carve in white marble. Her more discerning audiences often felt that she gave them a cultural experience as well as a hard-on.

The manager's notion was that artistic and cultural performances were something in which Mineral Point was conspicuously lacking. Some of the California gold towns had whole opera houses made of marble. Here the Silver Spur had the high-rolling gamblers, and Hellgate Hanna's had the best selection of daughters of joy. It was only fitting that the third top-rate establishment in town, the saloon of the Hotel San Juan, should have its specialty too.

The posters announcing this coming event had caused an expectant stir in the town. After all, it was not every day that "a great European soprano" and her "noble-born accompanist on the piano, Baron von Graffstein" came to a place like Mineral Point. The hotel manager approved of the baron, too. The nobleman was tall, stooped, cadaverous, and thin-blooded—the way people in Colorado expected noblemen to be.

All in all, the manager was highly pleased and saw to it that Madame Avellan was given the hotel's front corner room at the other end of the building from Doc's room. She said it wouldn't do. When told it was the finest hotel room in Mineral Point, she wept and demanded to be shown Doc's room.

Doc was reasonably tidy, but there's something about a man's stay in a room, along with his cheroots and whiskey, which can make a woman feel the accommodations previously offered to her were superior in comparison.

"Do come back and see me again," Doc told her as she left after her tour of inspection. "By the way, have you seen Room 23?"

She paused in the doorway. "No, I haven't. Maybe I would like it." She turned to the harassed porter. "Why didn't you mention Room 23 to me?"

"Lady, it's—"

"Show it to me! Now! Now!"

"Look—"

"I want to see it. I have been promised the best room in the hotel." She stamped her foot. "Show it to me right now!"

The porter shot Doc Weatherbee a malevolent look and led Madame Avellana and the attendant baron, who remained silent and in the background, down the corridor. The porter rapped on the door to Room 23, listened for a moment, then inserted his master key in the lock and turned it. He pushed the door open, and Madame Avellana swept past him to see the room for herself.

Raider lay naked on the bed, pointing his big Remington six-gun at her. Clothes, boots, and empty bottles lay scattered about the floor of the shabby room.

Ouray looked at the sun. It was low in the sky, but he reckoned he had daylight enough left. He galloped away from the agency into the forbidden part of the mountains. Sweat foamed on his horse's flanks, and its breath came in great pants, but still Ouray forced it on over loose stone screes, through valleys, across the bases of peaks, through cool dark pinewoods, across sun-warmed naked rock, until he reached the place where the new balloon was hidden.

Arcady T. Harrison was there. Ouray did not care one way or the other. If Harrison had not been there, Ouray was fairly sure he could have managed by himself. But Ouray had already provided for the possibility that Harrison would be there. He understood Harrison. The white man would never believe that a Ute understood him, just as Ouray could bully and fool Major Wheeler easily because Wheeler could not imagine being mentally tricked by a Ute. Arcady T. Harrison was a clever and knowledgeable man. Ouray respected him for that. But Harrison was also a weak man. Ouray would make him suffer for that.

Harrison seemed less than pleased to see him, and after a brief greeting went on with his work on the paper folds of the balloon.

"You like life back with your people in the town?" Ouray inquired in a slightly offended tone.

Arcady looked up at him and smiled. "I never could persuade you to get me any Indian women while we were out here."

"You do less work now that you have women and whiskey."

"I'm working," Harrison said indignantly. "Look at this new balloon."

"When will it be ready to fly?"

"It's ready right now. I'm going to send it up tomorrow. These are just some finishing touches I'm adding to it."

Ouray walked away, and Harrison went back to work. In a few minutes Ouray returned, carrying jars of different colored paints.

Harrison glanced up and said, "Forget that, Ouray. We'll do it on the next one instead."

Ouray was unperturbed and set about opening the jars.

"Did you hear me, Ouray? I said I don't want any of your Indian designs on this balloon."

"If you want to fly it over Ute country, it must first be a Ute balloon."

Harrison laughed. "Whatever you say, Chief. But I never thought I'd see an Indian use warpaint bought in Shultz's Hardware Store."

Ouray did not respond to this and went about his task of painting the balloon. He was not "decorating" the balloon, as Harrison thought. In fact, it had taken Ouray a long time to understand that the white man's "decorations" meant nothing and were there just to please the eye. Ute figures and designs had meanings. Ouray was not a medicine man and so could not explain exactly the significance of the design of big eyes and fierce teeth—but every Ute, even young children, knew what they represented, a soul-devouring spirit from the forbidden part of the mountains in which they now were.

Harrison was interested to see that this was exactly the same design as the previous one that Ouray had made, and he began to think that maybe it was not simply some slap-dash version of a Halloween joke.

When Ouray had finished, he surveyed his work carefully. "It will do. I will go up. You stay here."

Harrison started in surprise. "Neither of us is going anywhere this evening. It's going to be dark in a short while. And this balloon was not made for a joyride. I'm going to perform my first serious tests with it tomorrow. You're welcome to come along then if you like."

"I will go up now," Ouray said. "Alone."

"No!"

Ouray looked down at Harrison fiercely. The little man was adamant, and did not back off.

Ouray pulled out the wad of government dollars he had

received from Major Wheeler. He handed the money to Harrison. "You spend this on your woman and whiskey."

Harrison fingered through the money in amazement.

"Hurry," Ouray told him. "The sun will soon be setting. I will help you ready the balloon."

Arcady stuffed the money in his pocket.

Ouray smiled. He had been right about this man. Harrison was weak.

Some of the wet scarlet, black, and white paint smeared on its brown background, but all in all Ouray was pleased with the appearance of the big globe that hovered at five times a man's height above the ground, tethered on a length of rope.

With a nod to Harrison, Ouray single-handedly hauled down the balloon by the rope until he could rush over to climb in the wickerwork basket suspended beneath it. The whole contraption again rose quickly into the air, and the basket wobbled precariously as the big Ute made himself comfortable in it.

Arcady T. Harrison had mixed feelings as he saw his creation about to leave in what he knew would be a doomed flight at the hands of Ouray. Ballooning in gathering darkness among these sheer rock faces and jagged peaks would be suicidal for even an experienced aeronaut. Perhaps this might be a way of solving the problem of Ouray. Arcady put this ignoble thought out of his mind, with a lingering memory that Ouray's death on this balloon flight might indeed be timely. Calvin Thornton had paid Arcady a visit and forced him to reveal his plans for the balloon transportation of ore. So there was no longer any need to test the balloons secretly in uninhabited Ute country. In fact, although he had not told Ouray so, Arcady had been preparing this balloon as a demonstration model for Thornton in order to get more cash from him. With Ouray's money now in hand, this was no longer necessary. He could build another balloon anytime he wanted. Tonight he would hit town with his newfound funds, and he and Laura would have a high old time. To hell with tomorrow. And the day after.

First of all, Arcady had to get this crazy Ute chief airborne. If the damn balloon took Ouray all the way across Kansas and into Missouri, that'd be just fine so far as Arcady was concerned.

The balloon was tethered by a knot about a third of the way along the total length of a long heavy rope. When its ascent had fully tautened this third of the rope, Harrison released the knot and uncoiled the rope from around a heavy boulder. The balloon immediately glided away eastward, trailing the full length of the thick rope behind it and with its passenger suspended less than thirty feet above the ground. Harrison waited till the balloon disappeared from sight behind the shoulder of a hill, then hurried to his horse and set off for town.

The sun was setting with a fiery orange and red glow as the balloon drifted into a long valley with many Ute encampments. The children saw it first. They ran screaming to their family teepees, from which their mothers emerged. The women took one look and dived back inside. Men armed with rifles emerged from under the flaps of the teepees and came forward in a band to meet the intruder.

The rays of the setting sun added a fiery hue to the balloon and its fierce design. Beneath this soul-destroyer from the forbidden mountains, they could see a ghostly flame flicker. In the gathering darkness, the flames of the oil burner gave an internal glow to the hollow structure above and also illuminated the solitary figure who stood with dignity in the basket beneath.

"Ouray!"

"It's Ouray!"

Ouray heard their shouts and raised his right hand in greeting. He knew that the major test of his plan was at hand. Would they believe that he had returned from the dead to attack them with this soul-devourer? Or would they see him as a great chief who had lived with the spirits during his disappearance after being attacked by Mr. Hot Stuff and who now had broken and tamed this soul-devourer and used it as his horse?

Ouray put the questions more simply: Would they now shoot at him with their rifles and kill him? Or would they accept him as a divine messenger? He would soon know.

Ouray was certain of one thing—that the Utes would be impressed. Harrison had told him about the people outside Paris attacking the downed balloon with pitchforks, thinking they had killed a monstrous demon. Ouray himself had seen Raider's reaction—the white gunfighter had gone on the attack without hesitation, believing also that he was seeing some living or undead creature. Ouray was betting that the big difference with his own people would be that they would not attack what they regarded as a member of the Ute spirit world. If a spirit was evil, a human fled it. Only a very great medicine man could struggle with a member of the spirit world—and then only after fasting and being alone for many days in a desolate place.

Ouray had thought all these things. Soon now he would know them or die. That was the way of a great chief.

As the glowing soul-devourer, bearing Ouray beneath it, glided silently through the dusk toward them, the shouts of the men died down. They began to back away to each side as the destroyer spirit neared them. They let the thing see they were throwing down their guns and letting it pass unmolested. Ouray continued to greet them in silence with his upraised right hand. They had never seen him so full of dignity and power before.

The men had a further anxious moment as the soul-devourer swept over their teepees, over their unprotected women and children. But they could see that Ouray made the thing move onward without harming anyone, as it certainly would have done had Ouray not been its master.

The men in the succeeding encampments saw that the soul-devourer had not harmed anyone in the first encampment, and they too threw down their weapons and let the thing pass. They watched the fire of the thing glowing on Ouray's face and wondered at his courage. Ouray made the destroyer spirit pass over them all without stealing the souls of even the very old ones among them.

Men, women and children rushed to follow the thing to see what it would do and where it was taking Ouray. They ran after it as it glided down the valley, dragging its long tail over the ground behind it. Some of the young warriors, to show they feared nothing, ran forward and touched coup with a lance or stick on the thing's tail hissing through the grass. They knew if it just once brushed against their flesh that they would die. Others were not foolhardy enough— although they would have single-handedly fought a grizzly or a buffalo, they could not bring themselves to show disrespect for even an evil spirit.

Ouray was transported in this manner for the entire length of the valley, and as he looked back at the great crowd of his people following in fascination and dread, he forgot to make adjustments to the balloon as he reached the place where two hills touched and the valley ended.

The wickerwork basket was first to hit the sloping wall of the valley, forcibly knocking Ouray to its floor. The paper material of the balloon blew against the hillside and sagged within reach of the oil burner's flames. Great streaks of fire ran up the surface of the sphere for a few seconds, before the paper literally vanished in a sea of flames.

Ouray tumbled out of the wickerwork basket. He was too stunned to run, in spite of the painful heat of the fire above his head which was now descending upon him. Dazed, he managed to walk unscathed out of the conflagration.

The Ute people who had run after the soul-devourer saw with awe how Ouray killed the thing at the end of the valley. They saw how he walked unharmed out of the burning hell of the stricken spirit. They saw how he emerged from the flames, looked at them in great wisdom, and spoke to them.

Ouray could barely focus his eyes enough to see the great crowd standing there. He sensed that they expected something from him. His head was spinning, and he tried not to fall. He raised his hand for silence, although not a sound was being made by anyone or anything there, except for the crackling of the burning wickerwork basket behind him. It was fully dark now, and his figure was silhouetted by the last flaming death throes of the soul-devourer behind him.

"I have visited the world of the spirits." Ouray's voice was clear and deep. "I have many strange and wonderful things to relate to you. . . ."

The saloon of the Hotel San Juan was crowded to capacity for Madame Avellana's first performance. The hotel manager's idea was that she should mount the dais specially built for her, sing a few songs or arias or whatever, then get off again before too long so she wouldn't interrupt serious drinking and gaming, yet draw customers in. The manager figured that those who liked her first performance would stay to hear her second, and probably by that time they would be too bombed to move anywhere else and so would spend their time and money in the hotel saloon.

Madame had bitched a bit about the old upright piano, but since this was the only musical instrument to be had in Mineral Point, apart from a few guitars and harmonicas, there was not much that could be done. The baron played some notes on it as a tryout, and a few who heard him said that the poor sounds were not all the piano's fault. The hotel manager did not worry about this, because it was Imelda Avellana's clear voice that folks would come to hear, not the piano playing of some nobleman who if he wasn't a deadbeat wouldn't have be to be playing the piano in the first place.

The singer strode onto the dais and raised her arms for silence. The baron hovered in the background as usual and pulled up a stool to the piano. She looked back at him and nodded, and he started to plink-plonk the notes slowly.

Raider couldn't make out a word she was singing, although his and Doc's table was up real close. When he complained of this to Doc between two songs, Doc said it was because she was singing in Italian; it came as a relief to Raider to know it wasn't because of her accent or culture or something like that. Her high voice was beginning to grate on his nerves when she suddenly gave over the foreign stuff and belted out a fine rendition of "Clementine." The audience joined in with her on "Red River Valley," she brought a tear to many an eye with "Greensleeves," and she closed her show to tumultuous applause with "Streets of Laredo."

Doc Weatherbee stood clapping along with everybody else and gave her a big smile as she descended from the dais. She looked first at Doc, then at Raider, smiled, and headed for their table. The baron tiptoed along behind.

Doc got into one of his fancy acts—the kind that annoyed Raider. Doc of course knew that such and such a song was from Rossini's *The Barber of Seville*, another from Bellini's *La Sonnambula*, one from Verdi's *Rigoletto*, and another from his *Il Trovatore*, and that was the mad scene of course from Donizetti's *Lucia di Lammermoor*, but what was the wonderful aria she had sung between the two Verdi's? He had never heard that one before.

Raider knew Doc was not being a phony. Doc really did care, which made it all the more irritating to Raider.

"It was by Verdi too," Imelda told Doc. "From a recent opera called *Aïda*."

The baron made one of his rare comments. "It was commissioned for the opening of the Suez Canal."

Raider had seen a canal, but he had never seen an opera. He tried to imagine how an opera might be connected to the opening of a canal, and failed. But he kept his mouth shut about it so as not to look foolish, while Doc babbled on about all the wonderful things he had seen and heard in Boston while growing up there and later in New York City. All Raider could remember back in Viola, Arkansas, was hymn singing to a wheezy old pedal organ, and he had never cared much for that.

Men passing the table stopped frequently to compliment the singer with a few words. The hotel manager had been right in his guess that Mineral Point had room for culture. Everyone was on his best behavior, and Raider idly wondered if this was going to last the full three weeks of her engagement. Arcady T. Harrison came across to pay his respects. Raider had noticed him earlier, sitting at a table with Laura Winton. To Raider's surprise, the little inventor sat down uninvited at their table next to Imelda. He ignored everyone else at the table and tried to dominate the conversation with talk of his inventions and the balloon transporation of silver ore. Laura was left alone at her table, and she was casting some burningly meaningful looks across at her escort. However, Harrison was too busy trying to catch Imelda Avellana's eye to notice Laura's resentment.

Imelda herself solved the problem unwittingly when she turned to Arcady and said, "What balloons? What are you talking about? What do children's toys like balloons have to do with music? I haven't the faintest idea what you've been going on about."

At this point Raider excused himself and left. An evening of this kind of talk, with three more performances of Imelda

Avellana yet to come, was enough to lose the Hotel San Juan saloon this customer.

"I'm convinced my room is better than yours," Imelda told Doc when he invited her to his room. They had left the saloon after her fourth performance, which was greeted as enthusiastically, if more rowdily, as her first.

"I've never been in your room," Doc said wistfully.

"If you insist," she answered playfully.

The room smelled of lavender or lilac, Doc was not sure which was which, but otherwise seemed to him much like his own. He was in no mood to linger over furnishings. It had been a long and difficult courtship this evening. Doc in fact sympathized with Raider's viewpoint more than the latter would have thought, but Doc also wanted the lady. Harrison's botched attempt to take Imelda from Doc had been one of the high points of the night, for the inventor hadn't taken the singer's hints that she was interested in neither him nor his balloons but had persevered in his attentions till he had two women mad at him—Imelda because he was bothering her, and Laura because he was not bothering with her. On top of this, Harrison became drunk and tried to sing himself. That was when he was thrown out.

Imelda was wasting no time. Maybe it was the excitement of singing and the adulation of her male audience that had turned her on. She grabbed Doc's belt buckle and undid it while he was bestowing a gentlemanly kiss upon her. Then he kissed her full on the lips and pushed his tongue deep within her mouth, while his hands ran over the contours of her hips and squeezed the cheeks of her shapely ass. He had a hell of a time getting off her fashionable concert dress and all its lace underskirts, particularly because Imelda had a hold on his dick and stooped every so often to add her tongue to the soft stroking of her fingers.

Finally he bared her beautiful flesh, laid her on the bed,

and ran his hands greedily over her silky skin. His fingers stroked her bush and felt its moist yielding slit. He ran his fingertips just inside the lips of her vulva until she became so hungry for more she pressed her hips forward. His long middle finger sank into her trembling pulsing cunt, while his forefinger and thumb softly kneaded her erectile clit.

She lay back on the back, moaning and giving herself over totally to the sensations his expert fingers were sending through her body. Her eyes were shut tight, and she breathed between clenched teeth. She groaned as Doc's fingers glided over the soft inner folds of her sex and as he teased and squeezed the fleshy button that triggered passion in her flesh.

Doc kissed her deeply, squeezing her breasts against him with his left arm, and continued to work her into a frenzy with the fingers of his right hand.

She uttered a series of little yelps, reached down with both hands, and pressed his fingers deep and hard into her crotch. The liquid folds of her cunt contracted around his fingers in seizing wave after wave, and her voice was raised in a high-pitched wail that would have done credit to one of her arias.

Like the aftershocks of a big quake, after the Great Wave had passed through her body, its little sisters had their minor moments. She held tightly onto his hand and kept it stuffed into what meant most to her. Then, all of an instant, her hands dropped away and every muscle in her body went limp.

"Don't go away," she murmured.

That was the last thing on Doc's mind.

CHAPTER EIGHT

Calvin Thornton stood behind the bar at the Silver Spur, oblivious to customers' occasional attempts at conversation with him. He stared sullenly across the big saloon and took a deep pull every so often on a bottle of Jack Daniels Tennessee sour-mash whiskey. The bartender paid him no heed, and those of his hired hands who happened to wander in made sure they happened to wander out again after a single drink. Most people who knew Thornton even moderately well knew the signs. Cal was going into one of his mean streaks.

So long as Thornton was doing business personally in Denver, Pueblo, and farther afield, he remained a gentleman—in control, reasonable, rational, responsible. But when he spent any length of time in a backwoods town like Mineral Point, sooner or later he began to revert to the wild. He never let his appearance go. His clothes were clean and pressed, he had shaved that morning, his boots were shined, and his hair was combed. It was the man inside that ran amuck.

His roving eye finally settled on one individual. Arcady T. Harrison sat alone at a table, waiting for Laura Winton. He was enjoying the recent news from the outside world in a copy of the *Pueblo Chieftain,* reading aloud choice items for some acquaintances at an adjoining table, who either were not readers themselves or hadn't seen a newspaper lately.

Members of the Women's Christian Temperance Union mustered a storming party of lady Methodists, Baptists, Presbyterians, and Quakers in a zealous attack in the war on rum. The first saloonkeeper to resist was told: "We have come not to threaten, not even to upbraid; but in the name of our Heavenly Friend and Savior and in His spirit to forgive and to commend you to His pardon if you will abandon a business so damaging to our hearts and homes. Let us pray!" The saloonkeeper looked closely at this crowd of indignant, self-righteous women and recognized there the wife of the banker who held his mortgage, the wife of the coal and timber dealer to whom he owed hundreds of dollars, and the mother of the county attorney, and the daughter of his family doctor.

One of the men at the next table laughed. "They got him by the short hairs!"

"The thing I worry about in this war between women and whiskey," another said, "is that they might give in to the women on liquor in order to pacify them from insisting on the right to vote."

"Anyone who thinks that would work doesn't know women," Harrison said.

"Damn right. Give 'em one thing, they'll know fer sure they can squeeze the other out of you."

"Where will we go if they close down all the saloons?" one man asked in such a helpless lost voice they all laughed.

"Durned if I see it happening anytime soon in Mineral Point."

"Look yonder at Cal Thornton coming this way. You can imagine how he'd treat those members of the Women's

Christian Temperance Union if they came here hollering and praying at the Silver Spur."

"That son of a bitch would put them to peddling their flesh to earn their fares outta town."

That got a big laugh, which died down as soon as Thornton came within earshot.

Only Harrison was not laughing. He was made apprehensive by the fact that it was for him that Thornton seemed to be heading. He was not mistaken.

Although Thornton was no longer holding the bottle of sour mash, he was carrying a load of it in his gut. His pale blue eyes reminded Harrison of those of a seagull. Or maybe like camera lenses, mechanically recording whatever was in front of them, but definitely in some way disconnected with the personality of their owner.

Thornton leaned his hands on the table and stooped across it to look at Harrison's face. "Spending a lot of money these days, ain't you?"

Harrison shrugged. "Look at it this way, Cal. All the money you gave me, you're getting back in the Silver Spur."

"But I'm not getting what I paid for in the first place."

"I'm working on it."

"Like hell you are," Thornton growled.

"Cal, you didn't hire me to dig a ditch. You employed me to bring an original concept to fruition. That takes thought. Now, some men need peace and quiet in which to think, and so they retire to a wood-paneled library filled with musty books. That was never the way with me. I think best with a glass in my hand and a pretty woman on my knee."

"How about a gun to your head?" Thornton asked evenly.

Harrison swallowed. "I don't think that will be necessary."

"The trouble with you, Harrison, is you think, think, think and drink, drink, drink. Now I'm saying you've done enough of both. I want results. Know what results are, Harrison? They're what a man like me insists on getting. I think maybe you made a mistake in taking my money. I ain't some college-educated wimp who's afraid to get down and dirty. I got blood on my hands, Harrison. You shoulda known that. You ain't going to fuck me over."

"My good man, that was the thought furthest from my mind," Harrison responded, seemingly little intimidated now by Thornton's diatribe.

Thornton's cold expression never changed. Without warning, he flipped up the heavy round table so that its timber surface slammed into the hint of a smile Harrison was wearing on his face.

Harrison rolled from beneath the table, clutching his face with both hands, as blood pumped freely from his nose. Thornton kicked him in the belly, and the little man curled up like a fetus in his agony.

Two gunmen on Thornton's payroll appeared from nowhere and stood watching over Harrison's friends at the next table. His friends all kept their hands on top of the table so everyone could see they were reaching for nothing.

Thornton continued booting Harrison's body on the floor, but he had greatly eased the force of his kicks after the first one and was connecting now with his instep rather than the pointed toe of his riding boot. Harrison, howling with pain and pleading for mercy, half crawled and half ran across the sawdust-strewn floor toward the door to the street.

Just as Harrison was about to escape on his hands and knees beneath the batwing doors, Thornton thundered, "I want results!"

He booted Arcady T. Harrison square in the ass and lifted the little man off the floor so that he parted the batwing doors on his way out like a cuckoo in a Swiss clock.

The two hired guns approached their boss with congratulatory smirks on their faces as he came back to the bar. Thornton's expression showed nothing—neither satisfaction nor irritation.

"Casey," he said to one of the gunmen. "That little shit has laid his hands on more money from somewhere. I know for a fact he's spent all I gave him. That means only one thing. He's been selling his fucking ideas to someone new. Find out who that is."

Baron von Graffstein and Arcady T. Harrison sat at a table in the saloon of the Hotel San Juan. The baron observed the bruised countenance of his companion and said nothing. Of course he had already heard the whole story.

"I assure you, my dear baron, that although the risk is high—and, believe me, I am never one to minimize the risk factor—but as I say, although there is risk, the enormous potential return on a minimal investment, and let me repeat the word enormous in relation to potential return, makes strict horse sense for the aggressive investor." Arcady T. Harrison looked gravely at Baron von Graffstein, even a bit sadly as if he thought that the baron's very natural wariness and suspicions might deprive him of this once-in-a-lifetime chance to get in on a deal on incredibly favorable terms. He said, "It's basically a matter of getting in on this opportunity before the Wall Street mob flood the market and the price of shares goes through the ceiling. You understand how the market works, Baron. Once word gets out, price skyrockets with demand."

"Assuming that such a demand develops, Mr. Harrison."

"Precisely!" Harrison beamed at him as if the baron had presented some extraordinary insight. "You and I speak the same language, Baron. Every investment carries a risk factor. What is the risk here? Is there silver in these hills? Is there anything else in these hills but silver, Baron? Can I not arrange to move the silver ore from here by some better method than that used by the Conquistadores in old Mexico? Can today's modern progressive entrepreneur do no better than depend upon the traditional burro? What are the odds against me? Low, my dear baron. Why? Because I am in touch with the newest technologies. For me, the railroad is old hat. Air! In a single word, Baron, that's where the future lies—in the air."

The baron looked impressed but still reluctant.

Arcady T. Harrison graspsed him impulsively by the hand. "I know you have reservations, Baron. I would regard it as a favor if you would communicate them to me. You see, I tend to be overcome with the huge potential of my project and overlook the minor objections which can be raised. You will do me a service by pointing out discrepancies or points unraised in my presentation. Believe me, sir, it is only by hearing contrary opinions that I can properly present the reality and promise of this great project."

"Well," the baron began hesitantly, "it's not exactly your presentation that gives me pause. To be quite frank, although Imelda depends totally on my advice for her investments, I always do her the courtesy of consulting her first."

"Understood, my dear fellow," Arcady said in as mellow a voice as possible. "By the way, I would certainly like to renew my acquaintance with Madame Avellana."

The baron smiled slightly. "That may not be the decisive factor in any business arrangement we come to."

"I didn't think it would be, Baron von Graffstein. I took it as understood there would be some . . . ah, private fee due to you. A confidential commission, you might say."

"Ten percent."

"High, Baron. High."

"What do you suggest?"

Arcady T. Harrison's face was wreathed in self-pity. "Creative people have to learn, Baron, that conceptual genius alone is rarely enough to give birth to their visions.

Therefore they have to be generous in rewarding those who come to their aid. I subscribe wholeheartedly to this. But ten percent is outrageous. Are you condemning me to die in a garret, sir? Five percent is the most I'll consider as an American artist and inventor, sir."

"Split the difference?"

"Done."

"Seven and a half it is then," the baron said, and they shook hands before touching glasses in a mutual toast.

Neither of them noticed the slit-eyed, leathery-faced gunfighter named Casey sitting with his back to them at a nearby table. Casey overheard only parts of their conversation, and the parts he heard he did not wholly understand. But he did hear talk about money and talk about the baron giving Harrison money. He knocked back his whiskey and ambled toward the door.

"I think maybe we should pull out," Raider said.

"I thought you were having a good time here," Doc said, as they stood at the bar of the Silver Spur. "What's eating you?"

"Makes me restless doing nothing," Raider grumbled. "I know we got responsibilities to our client and to this little pissass Harrison, but he ain't in no danger worse than having his backside kicked. It's like we're hiding out here, dodging work, just because headquarters can't reach us easily by telegraph."

Doc looked at him appraisingly. "You having a conscience attack?"

"Naw, it ain't that. Maybe it is. I don't mind putting time in on something I consider worthwhile."

"Bullshit," Doc said. "You spent how long tracking down three prairie dirt rustlers and now you begrudge a few days of sitting on your ass and whoring and touring the saloons while you look after the man you yourself found after no one else could. What do you want—him to disappear again after you've located him?"

"I couldn't give a fuck one way or the other," Raider said. "I did the job I was sent out to do. I think you're using this not hearing from Chicago as an excuse to lay about idle."

Doc pretended to look shocked. "How could you, as friend and partner, ever say such a thing?"

Raider laughed in spite of himself. Doc annoyed him with his exaggerated poses and by his willingness to cheat while filling in all his reports and so forth, whereas Raider rarely filled out his reports properly and got blamed for it while he probably put in more time on the job than any other Pinkerton operative.

"Who says I'm laying about idle?" Doc said as he saw Imelda Avellana come in. "I'm a very busy man."

Tina Martin watched tolerantly as her older brother, Tommy, effortlessly heaved shovelful after shovelful of raw ore into the hopper. He grinned happily and almost thought-lessly at being able to do work that made him important because he could do it better than anyone else, and as he grinned the slobber ran from his mouth, over his chin, and down his bare chest.

Her father lay in the shade of the rock face, snoring into his white beard. Each day old Johnny Martin spent longer and longer sleeping, even after making a short effort. Tina had not fully realized how much the work was beyond him now till she had come with her father and brother for the first time to the family silver mine. Before this she had always stayed home with her mother on the ranch in Kansas while the men left for the summer to dig silver. Now that her mother was dead, they did not want to leave her alone on the ranch. They told her she could cook for them, just so she could feel useful. This was how they still treated her, although she ran everything at the mine and more or less told them what to do.

Tommy was obedient and sweet. Over the years he had learned slowly what to do at the mine. He needed to be told what task to perform, when to do it, and when to stop doing it, and it was necessary for someone to keep watch in case something unexpected happened with which he could not deal. Tommy had been this way since childhood—Tina never remembered him any other way. Even as a small girl she had watched out for him. The only thing the family understood about what had happened to Tommy as a three-year-old was that he had caught a fever and had run such high temperatures for days on end that "his brains got cooked."

Theirs had been a quiet life on their small holding in the lush Kansas grassland between the North Fork and Cimarron rivers. Her father had bought the ranch with savings from his days as a year-round miner, and every year, like a migratory bird, when the snow melted on the Rockies, he got the call to come back. They could have got by comfortable enough on the ranch, but as the days lengthened and the spring roundup was done, her father lost interest in cattle. Now his talk would get to be of placer deposits, native silver, black powder, quartzite, mineralized veins— and his eyes sparkled and his voice grew young again when he mentioned those magic words: gold . . . silver.

Her mother called it a sickness in him, like the way some men drank and others gambled. As Tina grew up, she even got to think that her mother enjoyed being boss of the spread for the four months of the year he was away. She noticed too that when he came back, they were overjoyed to see each other. Tina had understood the only half-joking comment of a neighboring rancher's wife who said, "I wish your husband would take mine along with him one summer. We both could use the break."

She watched now as her father slept and her brother worked. She was strong, but this work was too much for her, as it was now for her father also. Tommy, in his simpleminded way, recognized this. Their silver mine was the only place in the world where he could do things that others couldn't, where he didn't have to be careful lest he break things with his great strength, where people praised him and genuinely needed him, where they were not just being kind or feeling sorry for him when they said, "Tommy, do this for me." Those dang steers on the ranch were too smart for him, and he always got mixed up on horseback. The silver mine was what he understood best. Sure, he got mixed up here, too, but his father always pointed out what to do, and now there was his sister this summer. He remembered his mother. She had to go away forever. He'd forgotten why.

Tina's father drifted in and out of sleep. He was simply old and tired and given now to laying back and thinking things over. He never came to any satisfactory conclusions and knew he was just getting into useless worry. The girl would take care of her brother. The Rorke's youngest boy had been more than willing to look after their spread while they were away. No doubt he had his eye on Tina and the ranch. She could do worse, in her father's opinion. Not that she asked his opinion. She was a good girl in most ways, except she had a weakness for boys. For men, to be more exact. Well, she was strong-minded enough to know what she wanted, and he was never one to stand between her and that. The best way for him to get her to accept young Rorke would be to say nothing one way or the other. She'd have the land, and if this mine lived up to its initial promise, she might have a lot more as security for her and her brother after he was gone.

Beneath his half-lowered lids he saw Tommy take something to show to his sister. The poor kid had probably found a baby frog or something on the ore he was digging. Tommy went back and forth several times, showing things to Tina. Then she jumped to her feet and followed him to where he had been shoveling. She stooped for a minute, examining something.

"Go wake Pa," she said to her brother.

The old man climbed to his feet hurriedly as he saw his son approaching, in the hope he would not be shaken awake. But Tommy caught him by the shoulders anyway and shook him back and forth effortlessly.

"Wake up, Pa! Wake up!"

"I'm awake, son. See, my eyes are open and I'm standing in front of you."

Tommy considered this for a moment. "Tina told me to wake you."

"You done good, son." His father patted him on the shoulder. "Let's see what she has to show us."

"It was me found it!" Tommy insisted. "Me! Me!"

"Found what?"

"Gold!"

His father laughed, and they walked together to where Tina was picking among the ore. She handed her father several chunks of broken rock.

"I guess this is what they call fool's gold," she said, showing him she was not as silly as Tommy.

"I know fool's gold," Tommy said. "Don't I, Pa?"

"Sure you do, Tommy," his father said abstractedly as he turned the pieces of rock over and over, and tossed one several times in the air and caught it in his palm, testing its specific gravity.

"Heavier 'n a big fat whore," he muttered, forgetting his daughter's presence. "Look here at this dendritic structure." He pointed in the rock to yellow metal shaped like a piece of moss or a frost-flower on a pane of glass. He dug the blade of his knife into a yellow, malformed crystal, and the steel ate into the softer substance. "Tina, get me a small dish and the nitric acid."

The yellow metal did not dissolve in the acid.

"I just wanted to be sure," the old man muttered. He puttered around in the pile of ore, turning the rocks and causing small slides as he uncovered rock deeper down. He kept shaking his head and muttering, "I must be over the hill. I don't even know what I'm doing anymore."

Because he kept at this without pause, Tina finally asked, "What do we have, Pa?"

"Practically everything here that ain't gangue and silver, girl, is pure gold. I ain't seen nothing like it never. And you found it, Tommy. All on your own. That took some doing, and I'm mighty proud of you, son."

Tommy smiled happily.

As Tina turned to praise him too, she caught sight of a motionless figure out of the corner of her eye—a Ute warrior crouched on a rock with a rifle across his knees and a steady unblinking gaze fixed on them.

Mr. Hot Stuff's hunger made him lean and stealthy as a cat. His own people now feared Ouray too much to help him willingly, and he was too proud to beg from Utes or force them to provide for him. These miners had a woman in the camp, which meant they probably ate well. He would eat first, then kill the men and enjoy the woman before killing her, too. A useless old man, a woman pretty in the white people's ways, and fool whose arms and legs knocked things over, a mouth that hung open, and eyes empty as those of a bighorn ram . . . Mr. Hot Stuff watched Tommy carefully and noted his great strength. Then he straightened and approached the miners.

"I'm hungry," he said.

"Sit yourself down over there." Tina indicated the bench

and table of rough-hewn lumber. "We have a stew of deer meat and potatoes. It'll be ready in a little while. Do you understand me?"

"I speak good English," Mr. Hot Stuff said quietly.

He felt too tired to boast or intimidate these people. They in turn paid him no special attention.

"Know what I found?" Tommy said excitedly to the Indian.

"That's enough, Tommy," his father said in that special tone which meant Tommy had to obey and not ask questions or argue.

Mr. Hot Stuff ate a bowl of stew and then had two more helpings. He thanked the lady and walked away, thinking that these people hadn't asked about his face or secretly looked at it when they thought he wouldn't notice. Probably it was their being used to the fool that had hardened them to it. Whatever, he could easily find others more fitting to shoot.

"What are we going to do about the gold, Pa?" Tina asked after Mr. Hot Stuff had gone.

"I gotta think about it."

"I saw Mr. Thornton in town the other day. Maybe he could help us."

"Maybe," her father said shortly. He laughed inwardly at the thought. That was one snake in the grass who wasn't going to hear about this strike, he determined.

Tina shrugged and said nothing more. She could see this was all too much for the old man and he shouldn't be coming up here in the mountains anymore. As it was, she had been the one to arrange everything so far. That ore had been taken from the tunnel days ago and had been lying on the ground there all this time without her father ever realizing what was in it. For God's sake, even Tommy knew what it was before her father did. She would have to take care of this, too, she could see. Calvin Thornton had been polite and nicely spoken with her. He always raised his hat to her in town and inquired after her father. He was an older man, so she could trust his judgment more than that of a man her own age. His white hair made him look so distinguished, she thought, and she liked the way he looked directly at her with his mischievous blue eyes. Calvin Thornton would know what to do. She'd ask him for advice.

Arcady T. Harrison worked nonstop and at a feverish pace. Talker and dreamer he might be, but when he actually got around to doing something, he worked faster and longer and achieved more than the so-called man of action. Besides, he had his sore ribs as a result of Thornton's kicks to remind him to keep working. Arcady had been warned by his friends that Thornton would have him killed rather than be outsmarted by him. Arcady had done some clear thinking in a hurry—he'd give the rights of the balloon route to Thornton, he'd think up some kind of smelter to stop the New York financiers from dragging him into court, and if he stayed close to Mineral Point and away from Ute country, he would be safe from Ouray.

Accordingly he fetched his materials from their hiding place in the Ute country, with two of Thornton's gunslingers as bodyguards, and brought everything to an abandoned shack on a worked-out digging not far from town. Thornton could see for himself anytime he wanted that Arcady was working on a new balloon. On the strength of this, Arcady ventured back into the Silver Spur and was greeted with a nod by Cal Thornton. Arcady figured that when he demonstrated the capabilities of a paper balloon for Thornton and showed the negligible costs of making one, Thornton would be forthcoming with a lot more money for him. Meanwhile he would have to make Ouray's contribution last till then.

Imelda Avellana—that was what he wanted now. Laura

Winton had all of a sudden become a drag on him, an interference with the progress of his ideas, someone who had no real appreciation of him but who was motivated by her own selfish desires. Laura was using him, that was it! He owed her nothing. He had given her a good time. She had nothing to complain about. Now it was time for him to move on. Do something fresh. Imelda Avellana could help him complete this balloon project. He was convinced of that. Laura Winton was holding him back.

More interference came from that smooth-tongued Pinkerton gigolo Weatherbee who had the gall to present himself as a doctor of medicine. He was a born seducer and rapscallion—Arcady could see the man plain. He would have to find some way of sending the two Pinkertons back where they came from. In addition, they doubtless were spies for the Wall Street financiers. In spite of their word to him that they would keep his work secret, he suspected they were sending progress reports on him back east. And these reports would mention his dealing with Calvin Thornton. This was where he got his imaginings of himself being led away in chains, convicted of fraud. New York financiers didn't hire gunfighters, as Thornton did; they hired lawyers. One could be as dangerous as the other.

While he worked at high speed, wincing every now and then from one of his painful bruises and reviewing in his mind the various threats that hovered over his head, he concentrated least on the threat that was actually physically present and closest to him. This threat took the form of Ouray. The Ute chief had dismounted some distance away and walked slowly through the scrub, leading his horse. He walked deliberately across the unexpanded surface of the new balloon, each of his footfalls punching a hole through its layers and folds. The horse followed behind him, ripping and tearing as it tried to free its fetlocks of the brown paper.

Arcady howled in range and frustration. He struck the

horse on its left haunch, and it broke free of the tattered balloon. Then he charged Ouray and beat furiously on the chief's chest with his fists. The Indian treated this as he would the thrashing of a hooked trout—he let the creature play itself out, knowing that the more violent the resistance, the quicker the fight ended. Arcady stopped when his fury had subsided to the point where he realized he was hurting his own hands more than he was injuring the cable-muscled, big-boned Ute. He looked for a moment at the shredded remains of his new balloon. Then he started laughing hysterically and jumped on the balloon himself, kicked pieces off to the side, and tore apart the few undamaged sections with his hands. He suddenly stopped his insane laughter and lay on the ground with his eyes closed, breathing irregularly.

Ouray looked on curiously. He had never seen a white man behave like this before. Certainly the Ute medicine men in their trances often behaved like this, and now Ouray began to worry that perhaps this white man Harrison had some connection with spirits too. But then he remembered that white people didn't have proper spirits, only those that the missionaries talked about—and they were all far away, even farther from the San Juan than Washington and the President. Ouray didn't care about spirits that were this far away. He wouldn't care about Ute spirits either if they weren't so close by.

Ouray had depended on being able to control Harrison's construction of further balloons, having surmised that Harrison, left to his own devices, would never actually get the project in working order so long as he was supplied with money for liquor. This way Ouray figured he could make occasional appearances with more soul-devourers and other spirit forms, good and evil, and keep Harrison from using balloons to transport ore, thereby revealing that balloons were like the railroad locomotives people talked so much about—things made by the white man and not visitors from the spirit world. He had to get Harrison under his control again.

Ouray looked at Arcady, who still lay on the ground with his eyes closed, twitching and gasping unevenly. He walked across and kicked Harrison in the ribs.

When Doc Weatherbee and Raider entered the Hotel San Juan, there was a message for them at the lobby desk.

"Mr. Harrison wants to see you, gentlemen," the clerk told them. "He's waiting in the saloon for you."

Harrison sat at a table close to the back wall.

"He must be nursing a hangover," Doc said. "This is the first time I've ever seen him stay deliberately out of the limelight."

Arcady T. Harrison nodded to them glumly and served them from the whiskey bottle on his table. He looked hunched in on himself, and he had a cut over one cheekbone.

"I've got problems," he said.

"Of whose making?" Doc asked brightly.

Arcady scowled at him and looked then at Raider, who was leaning back in his chair with one boot on the table, looking not at all concerned about the fact that Harrison had problems.

"Thornton will kill me if I don't give him the rights to the balloons," Arcady went on, "and Ouray will kill me if I do. I want you to take me with you when you leave town."

Raider said, "If Doc has no objection, you can tag along."

"I'm not sure we're within our rights to do such a thing," Doc said.

Raider snorted, as he always did when Doc got into doing things by the book.

"You see," Doc explained, "we've been sent by your financial backers in New York to locate you. Now helping you escape from Mineral Point kind of undoes all the work they paid us to do."

"Getting me killed here undoes it just as well," Arcady pointed out.

"Precisely," Doc agreed. "Which would be why I think Raider and I, as Pinkertons, would be justified in staying here to protect your life while you are developing your project for your New York backers."

"What about Thornton and Ouray?" Arcady demanded.

"Obviously your agreements with them are fraudulent and invalid," Doc opined. "You'll have to give them their money back."

"How?"

"From the next payment due you as you make progress with your transportation system."

"If I live that long," Harrison said.

"We'll endeavor to see that you do," Doc said with confidence.

Raider exploded. "Why the hell don't you let this little asshole leave with us? He ain't worth all this trouble."

"Unlike you, Raider," Doc replied, "I have been filing reports. True to my word, I have not said in them what Arcady is actually doing. I think by now that headquarters is in a position to issue us with instructions. I intend to follow those when they arrive, as I urge you to also. In the meantime, until those orders arrive, I see it as our duty to prevent harm coming to Arcady and to aid him in every reasonable way with his technical project."

Raider swallowed his drink and poured himself another from Harrison's bottle, glaring belligerently from his partner to the inventor and back again.

Finally he said, "I suppose I can't just leave you two assholes here alone. It'd look bad if I left and the pair of you got drygulched." He pointed a finger in Harrison's face.

"But you ain't worth it, you double-dealin' shit, and if you give me a hard time"—Raider banged his boot on the table—"I'll stomp you into the ground."

Arcady shuddered with fright.

Doc said smoothly, "Good, I'm glad it's all settled."

He and Harrison began clapping when Imelda Avellana and Baron von Graffstein walked out onto the dais.

Raider cursed and started to climb out of his chair.

"You can't leave now without giving offense," Doc said and pushed Harrison's bottle toward Raider.

Raider subsided unwillingly into his chair. "Goddamn European soprano."

Harrison smiled. "I have my doubts about that. The baron's accent is definitely Brooklyn. And I think she might better be described as a Philadelphia contralto than a European soprano."

"Baltimore," Doc corrected him.

"You know that?" Arcady asked with interest.

"She told me."

A jealous look crossed Harrison's face.

The slow plinking notes on the piano began, and Madame Avellana's voice tackled a flight of high notes. Raider took a deep slug of whiskey and slouched back to wait impatiently for "Clementine" and "Streets of Laredo."

Midway through her second song, two men rushed in through the batwing doors. They were hissed and told to keep quiet, but few saw that both had their pistols drawn and had bandannas covering their faces. They ran without stop up to the dais, and each of them put two slugs into the thin, frail body of the pianist.

The baron was swept off the piano stool like a leaf in a wind. The force of the bullets slammed him against the wall, and his lifeless body slumped to the floor with his arms and legs stuck out at odd angles.

After shooting him, the two assassins turned immediately

and were nearing the exit to the street by the time the baron's body hit the floor. It was only then that it began to sink into people's minds what had happened right before their eyes.

Doc was on his feet asking Harrison if he had a gun. Harrison didn't.

Raider sneered at his unarmed partner and slapped leather.

His Remington .44 roared once and tore away the forehead of the lead gunman. The man spun around on his heels as if he were in some kind of dance, spraying a wide splattering of blood over those sitting at nearby tables. Then he fell as lifeless as an old boot onto the sawdust.

The second gunslinger tried a wild shot at Raider, and the bullet buried itself high and harmlessly in a wooden pillar. The killer took two of Raider's bullets in rapid succession. The first snapped the bone of his right forearm, causing his arm to sag in a newly made elbow and the revolver to drop from his nerveless fingers. The second flying piece of lead broke apart the muscles of his chest, snapped a rib into splinters, collapsed a lung, and nicked his aortic arch before exiting through his back and breaking a rum bottle on a table.

The gunslinger struggled on the ground like he was wrestling with some invisible opponent. Gradually his struggles got weaker. He managed to claw onto the leg of a chair, and he died holding it like it was the hand of the only friend he had left on earth.

Doc and others checked the baron's body while Raider watched the door and everyone else.

Imelda stood quietly and dejectedly upon the dais, with no sign of any prima donna histrionics.

Doc looked up from the baron's body and shook his head at her. He approached her slowly and stretched out his hand to her.

She backed off. "Thanks all the same, Doc, but no sympathy. Poor little bastard is done for. I led him a merry chase." She looked at Doc with sad eyes. "He loved me, you know. I guess he had to put up with a lot."

Imelda left the dais hurriedly, and Doc decided it was best to let her go.

One man was saying as he looked at the first gunslinger to get hit, "I couldn't say for sure who this one is. Too much of his face is blowed off.

Another man had pulled the bandanna from the face of the second dead killer. "We all know who this one is."

He didn't dare say what he meant—that this was one of Thornton's hired guns.

Doc looked at Harrison, who was deathly pale.

"I think word must have gotten out that the baron was about to invest in my project," Arcady told Raider and Doc quietly as the marshal took statements from various people. "But I'm not saying anything about this except to you two."

Raider spat. "Pity Thornton didn't send them after you instead of the baron. I'd have helped them maybe."

CHAPTER NINE

Mr. Hot Stuff dismounted and tied up his horse at a patch of grass in the shade of a cottonwood. It was easier to go down the rocky inclines by foot than by horse. The Ute warrior moved swiftly and with the least possible effort among the rockslides, streams, animal paths, tiny valleys, and sheer drops that marked the approach to Tahkoonica-vats' summer hunting grounds. He saw the first sentinels and continued regardless until he came out onto a level place with a spring of sweet water. Here he drank his fill and rested in the shade. The sentinels would have sent their signals, so he should not have long to wait.

He didn't. Tahkoonicavats came himself, which in a way was a mark of respect for Mr. Hot Stuff but in another way signified that Tahkoonicavats wanted to parley out here and did not intend to offer hospitality to Mr. Hot Stuff.

After the formal greetings were over and both men had sized up each other for the first time in three or four years, Mr. Hot Stuff spoke.

"My enmity to Ouray is well known, and I do not have to describe it to you. Likewise, I know you have no great admiration for this man. You and I, each in our own way, openly stand against him."

Tahkoonicavats gestured violently in denial. "Ouray is not my enemy. The white men he has brought to the San Juan are my enemy. You care only for your quarrel with

Ouray, and would use the white men and me as thorns in his flesh. I will not be used by you."

Mr. Hot Stuff did not bother to argue the point. "I'll use whatever means I can and whatever friends I can make. Before this, I knew you would not join with me. Now you must see how things have changed. The medicine men have held Ouray in check up till now. They can't do this anymore if the people believe Ouray visits the other world and has power over spirits. It's some kind of trickery."

Tahkoonicavats seemed uneasy and said nothing.

"You don't believe Ouray has power over spirits, do you?" Mr. Hot Stuff asked incredulously.

"I have not seen for myself the things that people describe," Tahkoonicavats said uncertainly. "But men I respect have told me how they saw with their own eyes Ouray swooping through the air like a condor with flames above his head and driving a soul-devourer before him as if it were his horse. That seems to me to be powerful medicine."

Mr. Hot Stuff laughed disrespectfully in his face. "It's white man's trickery."

Tahkoonicavats thought about this. It was clear that he would like to have believed Mr. Hot Stuff and that he believed the white man capable of anything. Yet if indeed Ouray had made a pact with the Ute spirits, Tahkoonicavats did not want to find himself allied to a man like Mr. Hot Stuff who had no standing and few friends.

Tahkoonicavats had enough of Mr. Hot Stuff's maneuverings. He spoke with finality. "It may be as you say. I do not know. None of us knows. If what you say is true— that the Ute spirits are not protecting Ouray and that it is a white man's trick, why don't you call him down in combat?"

Mr. Hot Stuff was trapped. If he refused to challenge Ouray again, as Tahkoonicavats suggested, word would soon spread of this all over Ute country. He would be treated as a coward. If he did challenge Ouray, Tahkoonicavats stood to benefit no matter who won.

"I challenged him before and he ran away," Mr. Hot Stuff replied.

"Call him down at Leopard Creek this time," Tahkoonicavats said. "There can be no escape from there. My brother will bear your challenge to him." He turned to his men. "Come, give gifts of food and ammunition to this brave warrior who challenges the power of Ouray."

The onlooking men cheered and came foward with gifts.

Although Mr. Hot Stuff could see that this scene had been rehearsed by Tahkoonicavats, he could do nothing now but swell out his chest and boast of what he would do to Ouray when they met.

Tina Martin rode into town every other day to break the monotony of the mining camp. Her summer in the mountains was proving to be quite entertaining. Back home in Kansas their spread was a two-day ride from the nearest town, and that little cattle town had none of the gaming halls, plush saloons, and houses of sin that Mineral Point had in plenty. Of course Tina had never entered any of these establishments, although she had been tempted by posters for recitals by a European soprano to visit the saloon of the Hotel San Juan. However, when she saw that these recitals took place in the evening, she put them out of her mind. She was always back at camp long before sundown to cook the evening meal for her father and brother.

She *had* been to the Hotel San Juan a few times with men she had met on the main street and in stores. She didn't care what people said about her—she was twenty-three and unmarried, and lots of girls she had been to school with had been married for six and more years. She had the same needs as they. Tina had stayed home because the ranch would be hers, with the understanding that she would take care of her brother and mother. Now her mother had died before her older husband, which just went to show how things never work out like folks plan them. Tina believed in living while she could. Circumstances had dictated that she delay in finding a husband, but not that she couldn't find a little love occasionally.

Cal Thornton had been one of her finds in Mineral Point. It had been a very casual encounter—a half hour on a sunny afternoon. Previous to that he had been polite to her, and when she saw him on the street at times afterward he had been the same. Cal was not a snickerer or a leerer like some of the others she had given herself to. Today she saw him sitting behind a desk in the small office his company kept on the main street. He was alone. His eyes widened in concern when he saw her walk through the door.

"No, I ain't got news you're a father-to-be," she said and laughed as she placed her heavy cloth bag on his desk with a thud.

He indicated a chair and opened the bag without much enthusiasm. He knew the girl was a beginner, and he spent a great deal of time with amateurs explaining why mica wasn't silver and talc wasn't gold. When these clowns did stumble across rich lodes, they often didn't know it till the assay came in. He picked some of the rocks out of the bag and looked them over. He stood rapidly and took them to the window to examine them in sunlight. Then he worked on them on a zinc-covered bench that ran along the wall behind his desk. Finally he turned to face Tina.

"So old Johnny Martin has struck real pay dirt at last." He smiled warmly to show her how pleased he was at her family's good fortune. "How much of this grade stuff is out there?"

"Helluva lot," she said gruffly in what she hoped was the right tone.

"I see." Thornton was thinking. "Your pappy sent you to see me?"

"Well...no. He hasn't quite made up his mind what to do yet. I was wondering if you might have some advice—you could give it to me without telling my father...." She trailed off lamely.

Another warm smile from Thornton. "I understand perfectly, Tina. You know I'll do whatever I can to help you all. I reckon your pappy is correct though in thinking that the best thing to do right now is to sit tight and say nothing at all till you got your tactics clear."

"And then?"

"That will depend on a lot of things," he said. "Leave it to me."

"You won't tell Pa I came to see you?"

"Of course not. You say nothing to him either. We'll surprise him."

Tina laughed at the twinkle in his blue eyes. She kissed him on the cheek and went into the street much lighter of heart.

Tina had gone less than a minute when Thornton stamped his boot twice on the floor. The hired gun named Casey emerged from the back room.

"You hear that?" Thornton growled.

Casey nodded.

Thornton held up a piece of the ore Tina had brought. "This stuff has such a high gold content, when they hear of it all the other miners will start wanting assays of their gold content too, even though they're getting paid well for silver. Casey, I don't want that to happen."

"Yes, boss."

"No one knows about this except them and us," Thornton said slowly. "Now if something happened to the three of them, who would that leave?"

"Us, boss."

"Think your goons can handle it? An old man, an in-
becile, and a girl?"

"Even if they did get killed themselves, they killed the
baron," Casey said.

"At the rate of two of ours for every one they kill, I can
expect to lose six men on the three Martins," Thornton said
sarcastically.

"Only if there are Pinkertons on the scene," Casey said
levelly.

"The Martins don't know those Pinkertons. Stay away
from those Pinkertons. Put two men on the job, Casey. Get
it done today."

Raider and Doc Weatherbee reclined at their leisure,
watching over Arcady T. Harrison as he constructed a paper
balloon.

"In the interests of science," Arcady said to Doc, "leaving
aside all personal considerations, I would have thought you
would have at least offered me assistance on this project."
When this had no effect on Doc, Arcady continued, "I can
readily understand the indifference of Raider to my project,
having seen his indifference to the beautiful music of Madame Avellana. I suspect Raider's thick skin shuts out all
the more sensitive and progressive aspects of the world. But
I thought you would be different, Doc. I thought you would
seize this opportunity to help mankind make a giant leap
forward. How do you justify your refusal to help me?"

Doc smiled lazily. "I'm not the one who took the money
and made the promises, Arcady."

"People forget that great artists and engineers have to
eat, drink, and sleep just like other people," Arcady said
angrily. "What do you suggest I do—starve and sleep in
rags under a bush while I push my work forward?"

"Sounds like you're describing the life of a Pinkerton," Raider said gloomily.

Arcady sniffed and went back to work on the brown paper. Raider and Doc exchanged a grin. They knew Harrison would work like a demon for another twenty minutes or so, then throw everything down and ask God to pity him and one or the other of them to help him. And on and on, until Arcady gave up and headed for the saloons. It was as if Arcady was happiest when his project was least developed. He seemed to have no great urge to put his system to the test.

"I'm going to ride out of town for a while," Raider told Doc. "I need some open country."

He knew Doc did not understand this urge. City-bred, Doc regarded a town like Mineral Point as wilderness. To Raider, the pressing together of people even in a small town became intolerable after a short while if he couldn't escape to the open spaces every so often.

"Now that we've found Harrison and Ouray," Raider murmured, "maybe I can turn up Mr. Hot Stuff."

"We're not here to do that," Doc said. "It's against regulations for you to go after him."

"Report me," Raider snapped and headed for his horse.

Raider liked the plains best, the way the land rolled easily away and did not push itself at the onlooker. First time he came to the Rockies, he felt as if there were walls everywhere, that somehow he was a prisoner. But over the years and much time spent in the foothills, mountains, and high plains, he had come to appreciate the kind of openness offered here and how it differed from the prairie. Yet he had never gotten used to towns.

Raider was being bothered by more than living in a town, and he knew it. He and Doc were getting the kid-glove treatment from Calvin Thornton. So long as that went on, there was not much they could do about him except gun down his underlings when they, on his orders, stepped out of line. This frustrated Raider. Doc had all his Pinkerton rules and regulations to fall back on, but these weren't worth a rat's ass to Raider. So far as Raider was concerned, Thornton was laughing behind his hand at them—waiting for them to leave town. Doc wouldn't tolerate any unprovoked attack on Thornton, and he was never fooled by any pretext Raider might think up. It sure burned up Raider to think of this joker playing games with them and betting he could outlast them.

If Thornton made any kind of mistake, Doc would move in on him real fast. Raider was sure of that. But if Thornton played safe, Doc would insist on going by the book, and they wouldn't be able to lay a finger on him. It might be a bit easier to persuade Doc if the person they were protecting were a bit more deserving. In Raider's eyes, Arcady T. Harrison was only a grade or two above a confidence trickster. Doc's line of fast talk was hard enough to put up with, but on this case Raider had two bullshit artists to deal with at the same time. With no end in sight.

A ride out into Indian country would be a welcome change from them all. Raider hadn't been really serious when he said he was going to search for Mr. Hot Stuff. It just seemed a good reason to ride out here, and now that he was in the wilds of Ute country, maybe he might happen upon him. Raider had not worked out in his mind what he would do if he came across Mr. Hot Stuff. He allowed things like that to work themselves out if they chanced to happen.

"Mr. Hot Stuff is afraid to fight Ouray!"

Raider listened to the echoes of his voice in the tiny empty valleys which ran in every direction, each bearing a little stream of tumbling, clear, icy water. He had climbed above the tree line, and his voice bounced off the rock faces like a flat stone skittering across a lake. The air was thin and cool, the sky was very pale blue, and the great jagged stone crags of the high summits towered all about him. His horse was pleased to stand and browse in a streamside alpine meadow, thick with wildflowers. Raider didn't really feel like calling Mr. Hot Stuff anything very mean today.

"Mr. Hot Stuff can't get it up!"

A bullet zinged past Raider's head and spattered off a nearby rock. Raider dove from his horse and pulled the frightened animal behind the cover of a large rock. He unsheathed his Model 94 Winchester carbine and levered a shell into the chamber. When he peered around the rock, he saw nothing, but there were a hundred vantage points for a rifleman in the jumble of rocks from which the shot had come.

Raider darted from behind the rock and ran forward to a cluster of boulders. Two bullets raised spurts of dust next to him before he reached the cover of the boulders. As he ran, crouched down low as he could, Raider caught sight of the rifleman behind a rock. He was fairly close. In a quick change of mind, Raider in his next advance did not seek cover but charged ahead, zigzagging through the shoulder-high rocks over the rough ground. A bullet ricocheted off a flat stone and made a loud whine as it passed near his left ear.

Raider threw himself flat on the ground and loosed off three shots that bounced off the rock behind which the rifleman was shooting. Satisfied he had pinned down his opponent, Raider charged forward again, rifle at the ready. He kept coming fast as he could, prepared to blast away if so much as a mouse stuck its head out from behind that rock.

One huge stride took him to the flat top of the rock, and he poked his carbine round behind it, his trigger finger pressed almost home.

No one was there.

Raider looked about him. There could be no doubt. This was the rock behind which he had pinned down the rifleman. Even if the man had somehow wriggled to safety, he could not be far off. Raider would find him.

Warily Raider remained on the rock, which served as a good lookout over the boulder-strewn area but which also presented him as a target. When he could see no one among the rocks, he eased himself from his perch and hunted along the animal trails among the rocks.

His fast reflexes saved him from the next bullet, which came from a totally unexpected direction. Again Raider caught a glimpse of his attacker—a Ute warrior. This man knew these rocks and was fast on his feet. Raider didn't care. He was going after him.

He charged the rock from which the shot had been fired, weaving in and out of big boulders on the way but never pausing to take cover. He poked the barrel of his .30–.30 carbine behind the rock, finger already squeezing off a shot at the foe he knew stood there.

The bullet traveled through empty air and bounced off a stone ten feet away. The rifleman had disappeared again.

Raider began to get sense. He was in Ute country, fighting a Ute. He might as well try to catch a fistful of smoke. No, he had to get the Indian to come to him.

"Afraid to talk with me, Mr. Hot Stuff?"

Silence.

"Are you a coward?"

No sound.

"I think Mr. Hot Stuff is afeared for his life." Raider laughed loudly. "I won't hurt you, little Hot Stuff."

The bullet whanged off a rock near his head. A second slug hit the rock next to him dead center, crumpled into a shapeless lump of lead, dropped on the rock where he stood, and rolled against his left boot. It was too hot to pick up.

Raider kept his head down and tried to figure out how

the rifleman could get from where he had last seen him to where he was now. It was as if the Ute was deliberately showing him that he could run circles about him.

A deep, fast-flowing creek cut off one side of the valley. This rocky corner of the valley was bordered elsewhere by high rock faces. The only way out was the way he had come in. If he allowed the Ute to get behind him, he would find himself trapped here. And judging by the way the Indian was moving about unseen, there was little Raider could do to stop him.

Much as it went against the grain, Raider knew he had to retreat. Fast. That Indian's next move would be to get between him and his horse.

Ouray was relieved when he saw Raider ease his attack and go back to his horse. He had decided he would have to kill Raider if he continued to charge him or even stay about in this place. He had no idea what had brought Raider to Leopard Creek, where he was to meet Mr. Hot Stuff in his challenge to the death. They were to meet at dawn, and Ouray had come this afternoon to observe what tricks Mr. Hot Stuff might be up to this time. Ouray had been hardly able to believe his ears when this white man arrived and called Mr. Hot Stuff by name.

Ouray had fired the first time as a warning. Any other man would have galloped away to safety. Not this crazy Pinkerton. He attacked!

Then Ouray had to shoot for real. He had two good reasons. First, Raider was attacking him. But that was not the main reason, because he could easily have eluded the Pinkerton among these rocks he knew so well. The main reason was that Raider was trying to contact Mr. Hot Stuff. No other white man in the San Juan would have attempted to contact this killer and scalper of miners. Raider might, and Raider knew how Ouray had used a balloon. If Mr.

Hot Stuff found out such a thing today, he would not fight at dawn tomorrow. Instead he would go throughout Ute country discrediting Ouray.

Ouray even expected Mr. Hot Stuff to arrive on the scene at any moment, certainly before sundown, and that he would spend the night in Leopard Creek, as Ouray intended to do. Raider might even meet him on his way out of the valley. . . . Ouray thought for a moment to follow Raider, then decided against it. The Pinkerton would head for Mineral Point, since he had not much daylight left. And Mr. Hot Stuff, no doubt approaching with much caution, even if he saw the white man, would not reveal his presence.

Although Ouray had missed Raider each time he had aimed to hit him, he felt the practice had done him good. He had shown how he could still move fast as a deer and unseen among these rocks. Many, many moons ago he had always been the best when he, Mr. Hot Stuff, Tahkooni-cavats, and the other young men who wished to be brave warriors hunted here. Together they used to drive deer up the valley till they had them trapped among these rocks. Then they would follow after them with bows and marked arrows, breaking the cordon that held the deer in. The one who killed most deer as they dashed among the rocks on their way back to freedom was the champion of the hunt. Almost always more of the slain deer carried arrows with Ouray's mark than that of anyone else.

Indeed Loepard Creek was where he had killed his first man, Ouray recalled. Not even a man—a boy his own age. The boy had pulled one of Ouray's arrows from a dying deer and was inserting one of his own in the wound when Ouray happened upon him. Before Ouray knew what he was doing, he had buried an arrow between the boy's ribs. Ouray had stood and watched the boy fall across the deer, and the boy began kicking too and clutching at his side at the feathered shaft that bore Ouray's mark. The chiefs had

believed Ouray when he told them it had been an accident—
he had seen the wounded deer run there and shot the boy
when he had seen a movement.

Ouray knew these rocks—every stone and blade of grass
and twisting path. So too, of course, would Mr. Hot Stuff.
It had been Tahkoonicavats' joke to select this place for
their combat, for Ouray had heard that he had chosen it.
He wondered if Tahkoonicavats was subtly favoring him
over Mr. Hot Stuff by choosing this place where Ouray had
most often been the champion of the hunt. Or was Tahkoonicavats taunting him?

Satisfied that Raider had gone and seeing no sign of his
opponent arriving yet, Ouray gathered up an armful of loaded
rifles and placed them one by one in hiding places among
the rocks.

He did not see the fierce dark eyes of Mr. Hot Stuff
following his every move.

Arcady T. Harrison offered to buy Doc Weatherbee a
drink in the hotel saloon after they returned from work on
the balloon.

"I'm to meet Luara here, so you might keep me company
till she arrives."

Laura Winton was already sitting at a table when they
entered the saloon. She greeted them very cheerfully, and
Doc guessed she had been there for some time. Doc intended
to have a single drink with them and then go up to his room
to write his reports before his evening meal. When Imelda
Avellana came into the saloon, Arcady saw her before Doc
did.

"Do come and join us, madame," Arcady said, rising to
his feet and pulling an empty chair to the table.

Doc gave her a warm hello, Laura a cold nod.

"I am so lonely," Imelda told them, "particularly before
I sing. I suppose I always feel a little nervous, and I always

had the baron's company to distract me."

"Time will heal that," Doc told her comfortingly. In order to ease her away from this subject, he asked, "Where did you find your new accompanist? She's very good."

"Miss Brown was a church organist and reads music," Imelda said. "She's a better musician than the baron ever was. Pity she's not a handsome man."

Imelda was pulling out of her depression rapidly. It was not in her character to wallow in self-pity, and she made no attempt to idealize her relationship with the late baron. Imelda was one of those naturally sociable beings that company—any company—always makes cheerful.

She was even willing to listen to Arcady talk about his technical ideas and need for additional financing. When he started into balloons, Laura exchanged a look with Doc and sighed. Doc made an excuse and rose to leave. Imelda caught his arm.

"Doc, remember you told me about that book you had in your room on Verdi's early operas? I'd like to read it now if you'd lend it to me."

"I'd be delighted to," Doc told her. Doc of course had no such book in his possession and had never discussed one with her. She too was making an excuse to get away.

Harrison seized her left wrist, pinning her arm to the table.

"Don't go," he said excitedly, shooting Doc a look of envy. "Sit here and listen to me. I promise you that you won't be lonely."

"Thank you, Arcady dear, but I really feel like reading this book now. If you'd be so kind as to release my arm . . ."

Arcady saw the look on Doc's face and hastily released his grip on Imelda's wrist. She left with Doc.

Laura gave Arcady a contemptuous look. "You make a fool of yourself, falling all over that woman."

Arcady was too busy looking after Imelda to pay attention

to Laura's opinion. As Imelda and Doc ascended the hotel staircase, Doc let his hand run down her back and over her wiggling ass.

At the sight of this, Harrison could not keep his face from twisting with jealousy.

Laura saw what affected him, and her sharp bitter laugh brought him to his senses.

Old Johnny Martin wiped his white beard clean of stew and grunted contentedly. Tommy was noisily eating yet another huge helping. Tina was cleaning and putting things away.

"You decided yet what to do, Pa?" she asked.

"Yeah, little girl, I been thinking."

"Well, what?"

The old man chuckled. "You're cut from the same stock as your mother, girl. Never a moment's peace."

"You haven't been able to make up your mind," she accused.

"Yes, I have."

"And?"

He cut a wad from a block of tobacco with his pocketknife and slipped it between his cheek and teeth. "I reckon you heared about them two Pinkertons who was sent to Mineral Point to find that inventor feller. I'm thinking I should hire them to guard us here while we dig as much of this ore as we can this summer without saying nothing to nobody. Then we hire every burro we can and bring all the ore out at one time, with the Pinkertons riding along. When word of the assay gets out, we sell the mine. I could never stop it from being robbed over the winter, so we couldn't hang on to it."

Tina was a little surprised at the soundness of the old man's plan. She had expected him to be unreasonable and, most of all, to try to hold on to the mine against all comers.

Cal Thornton was bound to agree, she felt, that this was the best thing they could do.

"That sounds real good, Pa," she said.

"Main thing is, Tina, don't you breathe a word about this to no one. Otherwise we'll have the scum of the earth down here hard upon us."

"I wouldn't say a word to anyone, Pa," Tina assured him. She was telling the truth as she saw it, since she didn't regard Cal Thornton as just anyone.

The old man and Tommy rested and watched the sun set. Tina was getting the oil lamps prepared, and nobody was saying much after the long day's hard work. They were isolated out here and had little company from other miners. Tina had always regarded this as a disadvantage, but now she supposed it was better not to have other miners dropping by all the time, eyeing everything and inquiring about the quality of the ore, as they liked to do. But it was lonesome out here, away from the general mining belt.

That was why she looked with interest at two men approaching, leading their horses over the rocky ground. She guessed they were newcomers to the San Juan out prospecting, although they had no pack mules. It would be nice, she thought, if someone started mining closer to them. There was lots of good ore for everyone.

"Pa, we got company," she warned.

Out of force of habit, the old man reached for his Henry repeating rifle and got up. Tommy remained sitting, playing with a grasshopper.

"Evenin', folks," one of the men said and touched his hat to Tina. "You be the Martins?"

"What's that to you, fella?" old Johnny said in a salty tone.

"We bin sent out with news for the Martins," the man said. He was shifty-eyed, lean, and itchy. His eyes took in Tina hungrily.

"This is them all right," his partner put in. He was standing well back, keeping everyone in his sight.

"What do you boys want?" Johnny Martin demanded, levering a cartridge into the chamber of the Henry to show he meant business.

"Now, that's a downright unfriendly thing you're doing there, sir," the first man said, moving forward. "Getting ready to shoot us like we was coyotes or something."

He walked directly up to Johnny Martin, pulled the Henry out of his hands by the barrel, and threw it away among the rocks, where it clattered down a slope. Martin had never even pointed the gun at either of them.

Tommy rose slowly to his great height, a look of bewildered anger on his face.

"Watch for the crazy!" the second man shouted, drawing his pearl-handled black Navy Colt.

"Why don't you folks just pack up and go on to hell outta here—" the first one was saying.

"We can't let them do that, Josh," the second interrupted. "This ain't no time to go soft."

"Don't seem right somehow," Josh mumbled uneasily. Then he drew his Colt Peacemaker. "Sorry, folks."

"The crazy! The crazy!" the second man yelled. "Watch for him, Josh!"

Tommy came at Josh, his six-foot-three, 260-pound frame wielding a short-handled mining shovel.

Josh wheeled about and his Peacemaker spat flame.

Tommy gasped as his body was hit by the .45 slug, but he kept coming with the shovel upraised. He swung down with the edge of the shovel blade in a mighty blow to the top of Josh's head.

Josh jerked his head aside, and the shovel blade caught him in the angle between his head and left shoulder. Like a mighty swing buries the head of an ax into the trunk of a rotten tree, Tommy sank the shovel blade into the gunslinger's upper body. The shoulder bones snapped, and the muscular red flesh was cut apart by the descending steel until the body's own thickness and density absorbed the force of the blow and the steel could cut no deeper into the vital tissues.

The second man fired his Navy Colt at Tommy's head and missed. Then he stared, motionless with horror, as Josh backed away from Tommy and staggered in a kind of dance with the short-handled shovel embedded in his left shoulder.

Josh let out a harsh roar of pain, which was drowned in a rush of scarlet blood from his mouth. He fell on his back with his six-gun still in his right hand and the shovel handle standing erect.

The second man saw Tommy coming for him. Old man Martin was half bent over like he was sick and the girl was just standing there, one hand to her mouth, while the huge idiot son, with a snarl on his face, bore down on the gunslinger like an enraged grizzly.

The pearl-handled Navy Colt roared twice, and each time the bullet slowed Tommy in his forward rush—but only slowed him. He kept coming and brushed the gun out of the man's hand with a sideways swipe.

He caught the gunslinger around the throat with his two hands and pressed his thumbs against his windpipe. But the three .45 bullets Tommy was carrying in his gargantuan body had begun to take their toll.

"Tina! Tina!" he called in a little-boy voice. "I'm dizzy!"

Tina pulled herself together. She saw her brother, as he choked the man, fall forward and bring him down beneath him. Tommy still pressed with his fingers around the man's neck, but the gunslinger was desperately reaching out now for the pearl-handled Colt, which lay on the ground near him. Tina saw him make huge effort and curl his fingers about the barrel of the revolver and draw it to him. She grabbed the nearest thing on the makeshift table and ran to her brother's aid.

The choking man, his eyes protruding, thumbed back the hammer of the Colt and twisted its barrel toward his assailant who straddled him. Tina caught at the revolver, but her hand was not strong enough to wrench it from his grasp. She locked the fingers of her left hand about the chambers of the six-gun, preventing the chambers from revolving and thus the gun from firing, as she stabbed wildly at the gunslinger with the fork she had hurriedly picked off the table.

It was a plain ordinary fork which she had washed after one or another of them had used it to eat stew. Its prongs were blunt, and it was small. She jabbed him in the cheek with it with all her strength, and its four tines punctured the skin and tissue.

She could not see her brother's face. His big hands were still clasped tightly about the man's neck, so that no breath at all came out of the man's mouth. His struggles were taking on a new power and intensity. Tina felt him pull the gun slowly out of her left hand....

She withdrew the fork from his cheek and stabbed wildly at him again. It scraped along the side of his forehead and left long red rivulets like a wildcat's claw mark. He broke the Colt completely free of her grip and turned the barrel on Tommy.

She stabbed at his face again with the table fork. Her move was too swift and his eyes bulged too much for his eyelids to protect them.

The four points of the table fork lay an instant on the surface of his left eye, touching the pupil and iris, before they poked their way into the fluid-filled eyeball. The eyeball popped and collapsed like a torn balloon.

Tina felt a swell of nausea rise in her gorge at what she

had done. She dropped the fork and pulled her hands away.

Some time passed, she could not say how long, during which she fought against fainting. When things were clear again, she looked back and saw her father sitting at the table, looking off into the distance and talking to himself.

The man with the shovel embedded in his shoulder lay still, looking a bit like a stillborn infant in a shroud of blood.

The man she had stabbed in the eye no longer held the Colt. His good eye was open, the pupil wide and unseeing, and his mouth no longer worked soundlessly in its efforts to find and swallow air.

Tommy hung on tightly with his fingers around the man's neck.

"It's all right, Tommy," she said. "They're both dead. You can let go now."

He did not. She gently moved his head on its side, knowing what she would find.

CHAPTER TEN

Mr. Hot Stuff shivered in the chill before dawn. He wondered again whether he should have tried to shoot Ouray the previous afternoon. That white man who arrived and shouted his name made him uncertain what to do. It was the same voice he had heard after killing the wagon driver on the Log Hill Mesa trail into Mineral Point. He had left then without touching the wagon passengers. Now he had not tried to kill Ouray from ambush. Who was that man? Why should this white man insult him by name? A brother or son of someone he had killed? He had no time to worry about it now. He had not killed Ouray while he had the chance. He must do it today.

Relying as much on memory as on touch and vision, Mr. Hot Stuff found his way in darkness among the rocks to where he had seen Ouray hide one of the rifles. He found it with no difficulty—a Sharpe's sporting rifle. It took him longer to find the next rifle, an old-fashioned needle gun. Then a Winchester...

Ouray still slept, breathing deeply. His eyes opened when a stone rattled among the rocks. He lay perfectly still, listening. His right hand moved out from under the blanket and clutched the Winchester repeater at his side. He sat up and looked carefully into the darkness, listening.

Although he heard nothing more, he had been awakened by something, he had no doubt about that. It might have been an animal or just a natural slide of a stone. It did not matter now what it was. He was awake now, ready for whatever it might be.

There was no sign of daylight yet in the east, and Ouray pulled his blanket about him to keep warm. He ate some caked cornmeal gruel with his fingers from an earthenware bowl. After a while he put his hand out to touch some of the sacred objects and lucky things he had brought with him—a medicine bag to wear around his neck; a bow he had strung and three arrows he had marked in the same way as when he had hunted deer in Leopard Creek as a youth; a small, tightly folded Star and Stripes flag given him by Major Wheeler's predecessor, the Reverend Bond; and other things. Ouray did not really believe in the power of these things, but he did not dismiss them either. For any man to survive and win, he must open himself up to all things helpful and useful to him. For a man to be a great chief, he must go even further—he must *make* things helpful and useful to him.

Ouray ate more of the cornmeal. He ate slowly, watching and listening in the darkness. He was not probing the night in a fearful way, he was more trying to accustom himself to all its variety of small sounds and movements—a breeze in a tuft of grass, water sounds from the creek, cries of night creatures, the sound of his own breathing, the beating of his heart. . . .

He saw the gray of dawn seep up from the east. He chewed more cornmeal and remained calm. Today is a good day to die. The Reverend Bond had told him once that this was what the Sioux warriors of the plains shouted on going into battle. Today is a good day to die. So it would be. He must not be afraid to look at himself on this morning which might be his last. The Ute medicine men said that this time before combat is the only time when a warrior sees clearly the man he really is beneath his weapons and regalia.

Fear is like a flame, Ouray knew, and consumes all before it. He had fought many times, had killed many of the enemies, had borne many wounds, and had known fear often. As a young man, he had sometimes panicked and fled in battle; that was before he really understood the warrior's life, and none of his people held it against him. Now he had tasted victory over his enemies too often to be restrained by fear any longer. He had come to accept a warrior's death in exchange for a warrior's glory while he could still kill his enemies. Let the women, children, and old men go about their peaceful ways. He would never live to be an old man. . . .

His death must be at the hands of a great warrior or against the white soldiers. Ouray sometimes dreamed of a hand-to-hand duel with the President in far-off Washington, of how he would kill the President and walk about this far-off place creating fear and respect for him among its inhabitants. . . .

But to die at the hands of an outcast like Mr. Hot Stuff would not be an honorable death. At this thought, Ouray's mood of introspection vanished and was replaced by a cold hard anger. He would kill this outcast who had challenged him. He would let the outcast's blood run on the rocks of Leopard Creek and stain for an instant its fast-flowing waters. Today Mr. Hot Stuff would cease to be a living man in Ute country. He would become a memory. . . . Like all of Ouray's other enemies before.

Dawn was breaking. He placed the sacred medicine bag on its thong about his neck. He unloaded and reloaded his two Winchester rifles and his two revolvers, a double-action Starr Army .44 and a shining new Smith & Wesson single-action Schofield .45. The Winchester rifles held seventeen .44 rounds apiece and would be the weapons he would most depend upon. He made three piles of ammunition, one for each of the three types of gun. Ouray performed these chores almost like a ritual, calming and disciplining his mind with the work and with thoughts of himself as a brave warrior and a great chief.

It was daylight. The tip of the sun's orange disk peeped above a naked ridge of rock, and the jumbled gray humps that had merged together in the half-light very quickly transformed into separate rocks of different sizes and shapes on the valley floor.

Some distance away, Mr. Hot Stuff stood, paced, and stood again, cradling a rifle in one arm and watching uneasily. Not for him the calm and dignity that Ouray and most other Utes valued so highly. Ouray watched him from where he was hidden and let him wait. The more anxious and restless Mr. Hot Stuff became, the longer Ouray made him wait. When Ouray finally stood up in view, it was not at the place where he had left his blanket spread with three piles of spare ammunition, his sacred and lucky things, one Winchester and the Starr .44 revolver. He took with him one seventeen-shot Winchester .44 rifle and the new Smith & Wesson .45.

The two men began a walkdown toward each other. They could have fired from where they were, but that was not what either planned. Ouray walked among the shoulder-high rocks and saw the head and raised rifle barrel of Mr. Hot Stuff approaching. When Ouray reached the hiding place of his first rifle, he quickly opened a barrage of fire on Mr. Hot Stuff, who returned fire just as readily. Both men emptied their rifles.

Ouray threw his empty weapon down, with the intention of picking up the hidden loaded rifle and covering a lot of ground unseen while Mr. Hot Stuff reloaded. Then he would rear up unexpectedly close to his opponent for a killing shot—or even if he missed, he would force Mr. Hot Stuff to empty his rifle once more and then he would charge him again with another hidden loaded rifle.

The loaded rifle was not where he had hidden it. Ouray looked about rapidly. He had no doubt that this was the place he had hidden it. The gun had been taken. Most likely, all the others, too.

Where was Mr. Hot Stuff? It suddenly occurred to Ouray that Mr. Hot Stuff was reversing his strategy. Right now he was probably very close by, ready to jump up unexpectedly for a killing shot. Ouray picked up his empty rifle and ran back the way he had come, keeping down and out of sight until he found a favorable position in which to reload his weapon.

But Mr. Hot Stuff heard the scrape of metal and bore down fast on him before he could pump the cartridges in. He was only paces away when he fired a shot, from one of Ouray's own Winchesters—Ouray recognized the blue beadwork band around the stock. The bullet whispered past Ouray's face and zipped off the rock behind his head. Ouray bent as low as he could and ran in and out among the rocks, with Mr. Hot Stuff following close behind, saving his ammunition.

Ouray made it to his blanket and the spare loaded Winchester that lay on it. He drove back Mr. Hot Shot but did not manage to hit him. Ouray now had time to reload his second rifle. He had two rifles against Mr. Hot Stuff's one and probably a lot more ammunition. Against this, he was pinned down by his enemy in an unfavorable position.

Mr. Hot Stuff lay behind one of the smaller rocks. Ouray could see he was lying flat on his belly and could find no way to get a shot at him. Meanwhile Mr. Hot Stuff could fire from either side of the rock without exposing much of himself to Ouray's gunfire. Each time Ouray fired, he had to expose his head, a shoulder, and an arm.

Mr. Hot Stuff seemed happy the way things were. It looked as if he might be settling in for a long siege. There was no way Ouray could leave this place without first taking care of him. The sun was climbing in the sky, and the day's heat was building. What tricks had Mr. Hot Stuff in store for him? Ouray was painfully aware that he himself had no more tricks. It worried him that Mr. Hot Stuff seemed content to keep him pinned down here. To Ouray that meant just one thing—his enemy had some reason to believe he was going to win if things stayed this way.

Ouray fired continually at the figure stretched on his belly behind the rock, trying to hit any part of him—but he could not. Mr. Hot Stuff did not waste ammunition, firing only when Ouray's head and shoulder were vulnerable. Ouray drew back and thought hard while he loaded the Winchester. He kept down and waited for Mr. Hot Stuff to make a move. Nothing happened. As he waited, Ouray's hand ran over his sacred and lucky things, item by item. When his hand fell upon the bow, it paused and then his fingers closed around it.

He selected one of the three arrows and held it in the taut bowstring. He looked out at Mr. Hot Stuff's position and could just see the heels of his moccasins over the top of the rock behind which his enemy lay belly down. Ouray stretched the bow, and without seeming to carefully aim, released the arrow. The bowstring whacked against the bow and the arrow shot in an arc high in the air, and high above the rock behind which Mr. Hot Stuff was concealed. The wooden projectile with its sharpened metal tip reached the top of its flight and dropped earthward. Ouray threw down the bow and picked up a Winchester.

The arrow fell almost straight down behind the rock. Mr. Hot Stuff leaped to his feet with the feathered shaft between his shoulder blades. Ouray fired the Winchester.

The .44 bullet caught Mr. Hot Stuff in the neck. It severed windpipe, arteries, and veins. Ouray had killed one more of his enemies. He was a great chief.

* * *

Raider washed down a mouthful of flapjacks with strong coffee. "You certain they were Thornton's men?"

"Sure they were," the miner said. "They weren't no miners. This is the first they've been seen outside town. You know them both to see them, I reckon — but you won't be seeing them about no more. The big half-wit son finished the pair of 'em real good, even if he got killed hisself."

The miner was having breakfast with Raider and Doc in the hotel dining room. He had brought the news to town earlier.

"Then the girl and her father are out there alone?" Raider asked.

"They will be soon enough. A few miners who know the old man are with them now, helping bury the boy. But they ain't fighting men. And you know Thornton will be sending more of his gunslingers after them."

"Why?" Raider asked.

"Beats me," the miner said. "You hear about people being driven off their claims in other parts but not in the San Juan. There's enough for all here. Everyone knows that. Maybe he's got something personal against them."

"Naw." Raider shook his head. "A cold-blooded snake like Thornton doesn't even know what a personal grudge is. For him, everything's business. I think I'm going to ride out there and take a look."

Doc looked up from his newspaper and spoke for the first time. "We have our own obligations in Mineral Point, Raider. Leave this to the marshal."

The miner laughed. "That no-good son of a bitch marshal says it's outside his jurisdiction since it's outside the town line. Be the same thing if it was inside. It would never be none of the marshal's business so long as it involved Cal Thornton. The marshal knows which side his bread is buttered on."

"How about the sheriff of San Juan County?"

The miner shrugged. "Maybe a deputy will come by in a week's time. Maybe not." He patted the Colt at his hip. "Out at the mines, a man's got to look after hisself."

"I'm going out there, and I'm going to nail Thornton," Raider growled.

"You ain't going to find Cal Thornton within five miles of the place," the miner said. "He's too careful. He ain't going to take no chances, not when he can pay others to do his dirty work for him."

Raider smiled. "He's been losing a lot of men lately."

"What does he care? Nothing." The miner inserted a slab of ham in his mouth and talked around it. "Hired guns come cheap. There's always young fools who think it's easy work."

"We been pussyfooting round Thornton long enough," Raider muttered. "I'm going to make him come out of his lair if I have to kill every gun he hires this side of the Mississippi."

Doc laughed and said to the miner, "He means what he says."

The miner stayed serious. "It's high time someone took on Cal Thornton. Everyone's so scared of him round here, they pretend to like him and say there ain't no man better than he is. They give him their ore and ask no questions, because that way they know nobody's going to bother them out at their mine. Raider, you better not expect too much help. I ain't no gunfighter. Neither are any of the other miners."

Raider nodded. "I know that. Thanks for the warning."

The miner left, and Doc put his newspaper away. "So far as I'm concerned, Raider, you're on your own, and you're making a big mistake."

"I expected you to say that," Raider said and left without another word.

* * *

On his way to the stables, Raider saw the unclaimed bodies of the two gunslingers from the Martin mine in a cart outside the marshal's office. The Indian agent, Major Wheeler, and the reporter-photographer of the *Mineral Point Gazette* were leaving the marshal's office, the photographer hefting his equipment on his shoulder.

"Great news, Raider," the major boomed. "Ouray has killed the renegade who was attacking the miners. I'm taking Bob out to get some photographs to send to Washington. They like to see that sort of thing."

Raider pointed to the bodies in the cart. "Are you taking a picture of these two?"

"Why should he?" the major asked. "They're nothing but nameless drifters. We're well rid of them."

"I agree," Raider said. "But I think it might make a nice newspaper story about who they work for—Calvin Thornton."

The photographer lowered his voice. "Be careful what you say, Raider. Anyway, Thornton owns sixty percent of the *Gazette*, so that kills your news story right there. Besides, folks prefer to read about dead Indians."

"Absolutely," Major Wheeler said without a trace of irony.

"Thornton may end up in your rag yet," Raider bellowed. "'Specially if I get my hands on him. I'm going out to help that old man and his daughter right now, and if Thornton shows his silver-maned head out that way, I'll remove it from his shoulders."

The reporter looked impressed and very nervous at this kind of loud talk on the street in Mineral Point.

When Raider arrived at the Martin mine, more than an hour later, Tina and Johnny Martin and half a dozen friends had just returned from putting Tommy in the ground in the graveyard outside Mineral Point. Tina was preparing food and the men were drinking whiskey.

Raider told the old man he was sorry for his trouble.

"Yeah, a wife and son gone with hardly no time between them," Johnny said. "'Tain't me so much as Tina, 'cause way I feel I'm soon going to be joining them and leaving the little girl all alone in the world."

"Shut up, Pa," Tina said, trying to be cheerful as she stirred a pot of beans.

"This here's one of them Pinkertons I was thinking of hiring," her father said.

"This is not going to cost you a cent," Raider said forcibly. "It'll be all my pleasure to take on Thornton and his goons. These men here to help you?"

"Two of them will stay," Johnny said. "They're brothers who have a middlin' ordinary claim other side of Red Mountain. I made them an offer this morning to come in as equal partners with me and my daughter, with them doing the work we can no longer do and protecting the place. They know the risk. But when they took a gander at the ore, I guess they decided it was worth it. They're nice boys. I knew their father years back. Hell of a miner, but a wild man for women and booze. These boys seem real steady, though. It's often like that. Old man will be a real hell-raiser and he gets church-going sons—"

Raider interrupted before the old man wandered too far. "Do they know Thornton's men will be back gunning for them?"

"They're good boys, but they won't make gunfighters."

"That's what I thought," Raider said. He decided he would make sure both these men knew exactly what they were getting into.

"I can still hardly believe it," Calvin Thornton said to Casey in his office in Mineral Point. "Fer chrissake, you send out a gun-toting desperado and he gets killed with a shovel. The second one gets choked to death by the same unarmed man. Neither of them has a bullet in them, and they went out to shoot a retard, an old man, and a girl. You want to explain this to me?"

"I can't, boss. They were both hard men. Something went wrong."

"You know how wrong things are going? One of the Pinkertons is out at the mine this moment to help the Martins. The big one. Raider."

"Christ!" Casey spat.

"You're going to have to wipe that Pinkerton bastard out. He was mouthing off about me outside the marshal's office a couple of hours ago. Saying he's going to get me personally. I don't want that kind of talk in this town. Usually I'd say hands off a Pinkerton, but this time it's different. He was overheard at the hotel this morning arguing with the other Pinkerton, Weatherbee. Doc was saying to Raider he was not going with him, so it seems Raider is not being sent out here by their people. They're real strict about the regulations, and Raider seems like he don't give a damn. I figure if this Pinkerton is killed while breaking Pinkerton rules, they'll let it go and not raise hell about his killing."

"Maybe," Casey said unenthusiastically. "But he ain't going to be easy to kill."

"You better find a way, Casey. If you don't, that bastard will see you dangle from a rope."

"I know it," Casey muttered.

"All right there, old girl," Doc said to Judith as he harnessed her to the Studebaker wagon. "It's been some time since you've had a workout. You're getting fat and lazy, lounging around here eating oats all day."

He removed the signs offering medical services from the sides of the wagon. He had no time for that today. He had spent time watching over Arcady T. Harrison at work. Arcady had a new balloon ready for flight and was performing all the minor tasks needed before sending it aloft. Thornton had no reason to shoot him now that this progress was being made, and Doc had already heard that Ouray was too busy acting the hero and being photographed with the body of Mr. Hot Stuff out at the agency to bother with Harrison right now. The one who needed his help most was that dang fool Raider, who was getting himself into a big gunfight for sure this time.

The trail out to the mine was little used and so was rough, but Judith felt so frisky from her long rest that she pulled the wagon willingly all the way. In fact, she was too eager and almost overturned the wagon a few times by going too fast when the wheels on one side were much higher on a slope that those on the other side. Raider greeted Doc at the mine with a none-too-friendly expression on his face.

"Look what the mule dragged in," Raider taunted him. "You in a hurry, or can you stay for a cup of tea?"

"I've been worried about you, Raider," Doc said cheerfully. "I've come to take care of you."

Raider snorted. "More likely you got nervous being in town by yourself and moved your ass out here before they shot you up."

Doc laughed. "If that's the case, then I think I made a terrible mistake, because I'm betting this is where the action's going to be before too long."

Raider was no longer taunting. "You hear anything in town?"

"Only that you were running your mouth off, threatening Thornton. But nothing unusual. Fact is I'm concerned at *not* hearing about anything. Could be the quiet before the storm." Doc looked at the sun. "Maybe a bit more than four hours' daylight left. I reckon they'll hit us before dark."

The others there listened in to this conversation and were not too reassured by what they heard. These two Pinkertons seemed a mite too casual to know what they were doing.

Raider introduced Doc all around. The group of defenders was reduced now to old Johnny, Tina, the two Pinkertons, and the two brothers, Burt and Jerry, who were the new partners.

"Are you fellas kidding, or you really think Thornton's men will attack before sundown?" Burt asked, looking as if he was having some doubts about his new business arrangements.

"They may attack after dark instead, or first thing tomorrow morning," Doc consoled him.

"I see." Burt was shaking in his boots.

"You want out, young feller," Johnny Martin cackled at him, "time to go is now. You want a share in this thing, you stay and fight. Make up your mind."

"I'll fight," Burt said.

"You're goin' to have to sound a hell of a lot meaner than that before I start believing you," Johnny told him.

"I'll kill the fuckers!" Burt yelled.

"Now, now, no need to use language like that in front of a lady," Johnny said.

"Don't mind that old goat, Burt," Tina said, coming to his aid. "The rules of etiquette don't apply when you're talking about Thornton and his men."

Tina felt real bad about how she had once trusted Cal Thornton. She saw that her going against her father's wishes in telling Thornton about the high gold content of the ore had caused her brother's death. Before the funeral, she had confessed to her father what had taken place. He hadn't cussed her out, like she kind of hoped he would. Instead, he had smiled sadly and said something about how everyone makes mistakes and how you can't blame yourself or feel responsible for all the things that happen in the world. Tina wasn't the sort to drown in guilt—instead, she wanted a crack at her tormentor. One in particular. A handsome dude with white hair, a white mustache, and cold blue eyes.

* * *

The mine itself was not hard to defend, being at the base of a mountain slope too steep for attackers to descend and too bare and high for them to start rockslides from above. With this solid wall to their backs, they had only 180 degrees to defend—which of course was still a hell of a lot. Doc unloaded guns, ammunition, and explosives from the secret compartment in the bottom of the wagon. When Burt and Jerry saw two Gatling machine guns being unloaded, they began to feel a lot better.

Jerry said, "I thought you two were loonies, in spite of being Pinkertons, by the easy way you were talking about taking on a whole mess of gunfighters, real professional killers. Now I can see you boys mean business. I never seen a Gatling before."

"I reckon you'll see them working before long," Doc said laconically. "Let's go to work."

Burt and Tina took Judith and the wagon to a high pasture out of harm's way where the Martins kept their livestock. Johnny and Jerry took the Martin possessions out of their shack and placed them in a dry pocket of the mine tunnel. Doc and Raider removed the windows and door of the stone-walled shack and mounted a Gatling in one empty window. The other Gatling was set up in a foxhole dug into a heap of milled ore. This gun gained cover from one side from the heavy wooden ore car on its rails. The ground sloped downward away from the mine, so their attackers would be at a disadvantage in attacking uphill. Raider burned off some patches of tall dry grass and bushes that could be used as cover, leaving the ground reasonably clear in all directions for fifty yards or so. Beyond that distance, rocks, hillocks, trees, and bushes provided dense cover for their attackers.

"I figure they'll sneak in as close as they can to see what's going on," Doc said. "Then they'll try to pick off one or two of us. So best thing we can do is get settled in our positions now, get ready, and then get down and keep down out of sight."

"It'll confuse them," Raider agreed.

While the others sorted themselves out, the two Pinkertons busied themselves with the black powder. Burt was assigned to feed ammo to Raider's Gatling in the foxhole, and Tina to Doc's in the shack. The two Pinkertons did not much care what the old man and Jerry did, so long as they kept out of the way. Doc and Raider had no illusions about their fighting partners.

"Don't shoot till we start," Raider said. "And don't get yourself killed trying to be a hero. I don't feel like having to dig a hole to put you in."

Raider was immediately sorry for having said that, remembering too late that Tommy had been buried only that morning.

"I don't mean to cause you no grief way I say things," he added awkwardly.

"You say it like you see it, Raider," old Johnny told him. "That's the only way for me. I sure hope these young folks is listening real good."

It was only after they had settled into their fortifications, Doc and Tina in the shack with the Gatling in the window, that Doc began to notice some things about Tina. First of all he had thought her just a tough kid, a little too old to be called a tomboy and a lot too well developed, with eyes red from crying, old clothes, and a coating of mine dust. Doc tended not to look too closely at females who answered this general description, preferring those in revealing gowns, elegant hairdos, and sensual perfumes. Sitting there with her in the shack with nothing to do, he couldn't help noticing her in the beam of sunlight that came in the empty doorframe. She had a long thin face, with a pointed chin, brown eyes, and straight brown hair that just fell any which way about her head. Her breasts pushed insistently upward beneath her dress, and her legs seemed shapely enough from what he could see of them. She was much older than he had thought, certainly in her early twenties. Perhaps a gem disguised as a pebble. Doc was further intrigued by the knowing looks she gave him, like she knew exactly what was going on in his mind. He talked and flirted with her and was even considering the possibilities of some hurried lovemaking when he was interrupted by a call from Raider.

"We got company! In the bushes and trees, to the left."

Doc kissed Tina on the cheek. "We must talk again sometime."

"I'd like that," she said.

She showed him the tip of her tongue through parted lips.

Damn Thornton and his gunslingers! Doc thought. They could have waited another twenty minutes.

"Johnny Martin! Martin! Show yourself. I want to talk to you." The man came out of the trees, his hands and the holster on his hip empty.

"Should I stand and talk?" Martin asked.

"Go ahead," Raider said. "I'll cut the freak in two if he so much as reaches for a handkerchief."

"Be ready to bite the dust," Doc called to the old man.

Martin stood up. "Don't come no closer. I can hear every word you got to say from here."

"Martin, I'm giving you and your friends a chance to sell out. We'll give you a safe conduct into Mineral Point tonight and out of the San Juan tomorrow morning. Go to Denver and sign a bill of sale there. You'll be paid a fair price."

"Who's going to pay me?"

"You don't have to know that. You'll be contacted by lawyers in Denver. It'll be all on paper and legal."

"You think I'd sell my mine to a man who murdered my son?" Martin yelled angrily.

"That wasn't meant to happen, Martin."

"Is that what Cal Thornton says?"

"Mr. Thornton has nothing to do with this."

"He's a goddamn lying butcher!" Johnny roared. "As for you, you're just a flea on his hide."

"You stupid old man, if you don't care about your own life, why not save your daughter's? A couple of Pinkertons aren't going to save you. I got thirteen men with me here, and any three of us could wipe out you lot in ten minutes. I reckon thirteen of us could do it in a minute. Is that what you want?"

Doc called to Martin so that Thornton's hireling couldn't hear him. "Duck down, Johnny, and say nothing more. Leave him wondering."

Thornton's man stayed where he was after Johnny disappeared from view, apparently thinking that Johnny was trying to make up his mind.

"I'd love to cut the shithead into pieces!" Raider whispered hoarsely. "Pity he ain't armed."

"Let's not be the first to shoot," Doc counseled.

The spokesman for the attackers turned about suddenly and ran for the tress. Moments later a group of men, all carrying rifles, spread and scattered into various positions on a broad front.

"I count fourteen altogether, like he said," Doc called to the others. "When they start shooting, fire back with rifles only. Let them advance, thinking that's all they're up against, before we use the Gatlings."

An attacker fired. Then another and another. The defenders fired back, but their return fire was not heavy enough or accurate enough to stop the steady advance of Thornton's men. They came forward, two or three at a time, widely separated, dodging from cover to cover till they found a suitable vantage point where they could squat and fire again. When they were about seventy yards away, but still concealed by brush and rocks, their shooting became much more accurate and Burt received a shoulder graze from one bullet.

"Time to give 'em a taste of your medicine, Doc," Raider shouted.

"Pleased to oblige," Doc called back. "Keep down, everybody. No point in shooting now."

Doc and Raider waited their opportunity, each behind a revolving cluster of barrels that allowed rapid fire without overheating. They had to make their first bursts count, because once Thornton's men knew what they were facing, they would not give the two Pinkertons another chance for multiple slaughter.

Eight or nine of the attackers rose in a bunch to charge forward and overrun their positions. Raider took them from the left, Doc from the right, both working clean across. Doc swept them with a hail of lead at chest level, and Raider cut across their bellies. Raider gave them a return run of lead before they could fall, and just about cut two of them in half and left a lot of parts of three others spattered on the nearby tree trunks and rocks.

Doc and Raider immediately put matches to the fuses running across the bare ground to the enemy positions. The black powder charges Doc had planted earlier all went off almost simultaneously and before the surviving attackers had time to recover from the shock of seeing their buddies cut down by the multiple-firing Gatlings.

The charges blew with bright flashes and great roars, flinging shale, dirt, and stones in every direction. One of Thornton's men was lifted clean in the air and hovered motionless for an instant—before his already lifeless body crashed down among the rocks and debris.

Raider and Doc charged forward, rifles ready, but they found nothing much to shoot. Bloodied, smoldering corpses lay about, some still alive but all beyond help. An arm, still clad in the sleeve of a red longjohn, lay dismembered at Raider's feet. The fingers moved a bit, like the legs of a crab long out of water.

They put down their rifles, and Raider helped Doc see to the dying men. Only three showed any signs of life, and they were all far gone.

"That's only thirteen accounted for," said the methodical Doc.

Raider looked around among the trees. He saw a rifle barrel protruding out from behind a trunk, pointing not at him but in the direction of the mine. Raider looked. Tina was standing in the line of fire.

"Duck, Tina!" Raider yelled. "Get down!"

She did. Fast. Too fast for the rifleman behind the tree, who now swiveled the barrel toward Raider. But Raider was too fast also. He covered the distance from where he had been standing to the tree in a half dozen giant strides and grabbed the barrel of the rifle with his left hand. He yanked on the barrel and threw the rifleman off balance.

Last thing Thornton's thug saw was the flash of steel as the 18-inch bowie in Raider's right hand swung in a powerful sideways curve that caught him in the solar plexus and razored through him till it knocked against his backbone.

Raider gave the blade a twist, to be doubly sure.

CHAPTER ELEVEN

Calvin Thornton stared glumly into a campfire on a mountainside. The embers smoldered under a pot of coffee, and the blankets on his bedding lay in disorder on the ground. It had been many years since Calvin Thornton had been forced to spend a night under the stars when shelter and comfort were in reach. To be forced into this by two Pinkertons who wiped out fourteen of his men in a single onslaught would have been unbelievable to him or anyone else in the town of Mineral Point only a short time ago. Now it was an accomplished fact.

Casey had come riding into town the previous evening with a wild tale of Gatlings and explosives, all of which he claimed to have witnessed with his own eyes from a safe distance. Casey had been sure the two Pinkertons were on his heels, coming to town to gun down Thornton himself. According to Casey, the two operatives had run amuck, laying waste to life all around them. However, even allowing for Casey's probable exaggeration—Thornton could not believe *all* his men could have been killed in an unsuccessful attack on the Martin mines—he deemed it safer to leave town until he could verify what exactly had happened and whether two crazed Pinkertons really were gunning for him.

He expected his henchman Casey back momentarily, having sent him into Mineral Point two hours previously in search of news. What could be taking him so long? Had they arrested him? Killed him? If Casey was in jail, would he testify against his boss to save his own skin? Of course he would, if he were offered a deal. He should never have sent that traitorous blackguard Casey into town in the first place. Yet he had to have news, and he could hardly venture back himself till he found out how things were.

When Casey finally showed, Thornton yelled at him, "Where the hell have you been all this time?"

Casey looked pale and nervous. "I waited for them to bring the bodies into town. All fourteen of them. They were a terrible sight."

"All dead! My God, I don't believe it."

"I told you I seen it happen yesterday," Casey insisted. "And just a while ago I seen all fourteen bodies, burned and twisted something terrible, stretched on the street in front of the marshal's office."

"What about the Martins? And those two Pinkertons?"

"Not a scratch."

Thornton cursed and kicked a flaming ember from the fire. He struggled to control his rage and think clearly.

"What do they say about me?" he asked.

Casey hesitated. "They blame you for everything. The miners were real mad, and I reckon some of 'em would have done me in if they wasn't sceered of me. I wouldn't give much for my chances if there had been more of them around."

"Do you think the miners would dare face me down?" Thornton asked, almost in disbelief.

"Hell, I think right now they'd lynch you."

It took Thornton a little while to stomach that, and when he did, he lashed out at Casey. "You damn lace-panty gunfighter, you couldn't fight your way out of a ladies' powder room! This is all your fault. I wouldn't be sitting up here on the side of a mountain if you hadn't screwed up."

Casey had gotten real quiet, his mouth was twisted to

one side, and he had a strange glint in his eyes.

Thornton decided to back down a little. "Look, it's no use us fighting among ourselves. What's done is done. Now the question is, what can we do about it? Are we beat? Hell, no. Not by a long shot." Since Casey was still looking unpredictable, Thornton went on, "We got to strike back. Hit them where they least expect it. Hit them where it hurts. Any suggestions?" he finished lamely.

"The two Pinkertons went with Harrison a short while ago to work on that new balloon," Casey told him. "There's maybe a dozen miners out with the Martins at the mine."

"How many men can you get together on short notice?"

"No more than five or six left in Mineral Point," Casey said, "unless some fresh drifters happen by. Give me a day and I could find you another twenty men in towns close by."

"Remember our motto, Casey—we pay in gold. That'll bring 'em in."

"Not too many have been living long enough to collect that gold," Casey ground out gloomily. "I didn't know they had Gatlings."

"Casey, they surprised us. Now we surprise them."

"How?"

Thornton slapped his henchman on the shoulder. "By taking the Martin mine behind their backs. You and me are going to be riding roughshod over those miners in a matter of hours, Casey."

Arcady T. Harrison climbed up on a wooden box and looked over a vast area of paper. He got down and in his stockinged feet carefully crossed the paper to patch a hole he had spotted. He fixed several more similar holes before he gave the signal to two youths he had hired for the day to haul on a rope stretched over a 40-foot scaffold. As they pulled, the paper carcass of the balloon was lifted off the ground, fold after fold.

"Hold it!" Arcady yelled periodically to stop the process so he could examine some area or fix a newly discovered hole.

The rope creaked and the unfolding paper rustled as the unfilled airship was hauled erect. Arcady shook and pulled on the rigging guy lines to widen and dilate the vast paper globe.

At this point Harrison was called away for a moment. It was Raider who finally noticed who he was talking to.

"That's Casey," he said to Doc.

"Well, I suppose Thornton expects to own this balloon," Doc replied. "You can't just walk over and shoot Casey because he happens to work for Thornton."

Raider grinned. "No harm in making him believe I will. Sometimes it helps if people think you're crazy."

"With you, a lot of the time they'd happen to be right."

Raider ignored Doc's remark and, looking toward Harrison, pretended to see Casey for the first time. Raider's hand brushed the handle of his gun and he got lazily to his feet, never once taking his eyes off Casey. He saw Casey poke his finger in Harrison's chest, say something to him urgently, and hurry away before Raider got there.

"What would you have done if he'd stayed?" Doc asked.

"Shot him."

"At least that's one thing we've accomplished here— shown that Cal Thornton scares as quickly as the next man."

Raider laughed. "I like the thought of that superior bastard hiding out somewhere, afraid to come back into the town he thought he owned."

Arcady returned to his work on the balloon, and Doc and Raider to silence and inactivity. In time Harrison got the wickerwork basket attached and, above it, the oil-fired air heater. The rope and scaffold were detached, and the balloon lifted off the ground, held down by Arcady and the two youths.

"Help us, Doc! Raider!" Arcady pleaded as the wind pushed the balloon, which in turn dragged the little inventor and the two lightweight youths nearly off their feet.

Raider ran and grabbed hold of the basket and single-handedly pulled the balloon down. Doc lent his weight to the other side of the basket.

"Hold onto it while I untangle some rigging lines," Arcady said. "You'd hold it steadier if you got in it."

Doc and Raider climbed into the basket, and the balloon immediately rose, bearing them aloft.

Doc looked over the edge of the basket and saw Arcady holding the loose end of the tether rope, no longer attached to the balloon. He had a grin on his face.

"You little bastard!" Raider roared and looked down the barrel of his Remington revolver at the little inventor already almost fifty feet beneath them.

"Shooting him is not going to help, Raider," Doc said in a calming way. "Gunning down the unarmed man you were sent here to find and protect—"

"I'll find a way to kill that little asshole yet." Raider holstered the big Remington. "Leastways now we know what he and Casey was talking about."

The balloon was moving as fast as a galloping horse and was now at least a hundred feet above the ground—although by looking down, they had the illusion they were standing still and the earth was moving past them. The floor of the basket bobbed beneath their feet.

"Reach up and turn that flame down, Raider," Doc said.

As Raider moved to do this, the ropes creaked and the basket wobbled on its lines so much it nearly tipped them both out.

"He's strung the oil burner deliberately high so we can't

get at it," Doc said. "Stay put in the center of the basket and try to counterbalance me while I climb the rigging."

Doc tried not to look down at the earth far beneath him as he pulled himself hand over hand up the guy lines running from the basket to the balloon.

"He's snapped off the control knob," Doc shouted down. "I'm going to try to put the flames out. Hand me up your hat."

"Use your own!"

"I can't put flames out with a curl-brimmed derby," Doc shouted. "Besides, it would ruin it. Some more oil stains and scorches on that old black Stetson of yours won't make much difference."

Raider cursed and handed up his hat. Doc held onto the hoop with his left hand, tried to keep both his legs twisted in the lines, and slapped at the oil fire with the Stetson. The flames were too high. When he hit at them, the downdraft of the hat caused them to lick up dangerously close to the lower material of the balloon. He had to give over and return Raider's hat to him. As he climbed down, the balloon lurched suddenly in a pocket of wind. For a moment, Doc's legs hung free beneath him as he clutched the lines with both hands. Then the basket swung back beneath him and Raider seized his coat in an iron grip and hauled him back into the basket.

The balloon was steadily ascending as it traveled eastward. Already they were several hundred feet above the ground and headed now for a valley between two huge peaks, beyond which lay another range of high mountains.

Raider looked disgustedly over the edge of the basket down at the ground. "Even that damn old mule and wagon of yours beats this for traveling. Hell, next time I come up in the air will be after I've sprouted wings."

Doc preferred not to look over the edge of the basket anymore.

Raider spat over the side and watched it descend. Next he pulled a cartridge from his belt, tossed it over the edge, and stared at it hustling downward. Then he turned to Doc.

"You know," he said, as if realizing it for the first time, "I think we could be in a piece of real trouble here."

"Are we still going higher?"

"Damn it, man, we're so far up now, another quarter mile up or down ain't going to make much difference." Raider drew his big Remington .44.

"What are you doing?" Doc asked in alarm.

By way of an answer, Raider pointed the revolver barrel into the interior of the balloon and squeezed the trigger. The slug blew a patch of brown paper out of the top of the balloon.

"Hey, Doc, you ever seen pictures of cannonballs making holes in the sails of old-time ships?" He squeezed the trigger again and blew another irregular hole in the fabric of the balloon.

"No more!" Doc shouted, pointing. "Look what's happening!"

The first hole Raider had made was now opening into a long rent down the balloon, and the wind tattered the edge of the torn paper, opening new tears across the paper panels.

"Doc, the ground's getting bigger!" Raider shouted. He looked over the edge of the basket again. "It's coming right at us!"

Doc stayed where he was, sitting in the bottom of the basket, looking mournfully up into the balloon's interior at the increasing areas of blue sky visible through the holes. He figured that right now they must be about halfway between floating and dropping like a stone. In another minute, there'd be nothing of the balloon left.

Both were caught off balance when the basket hit the ground. They tumbled out and then rolled away as the paper of the downed balloon caught fire.

Doc picked himself up and fussily dusted off his clothes. He looked critically at Raider, who had a slight limp.

Doc said, "I think one bullet hole would have been sufficient."

Doc sat that night with Arcady T. Harrison and Laura Winton for Imelda Avellana's final performance of the night. Earlier he and Raider had borrowed horses from miners with workings not far from where the balloon had crash-landed. They rode like hell for the Martin mine. Sure enough, they had arrived only twenty minutes when Casey and four hired guns rode up. Raider came within a hair's breadth of blowing a hole in Casey's head, and the frightened goon beat a hasty retreat back to Mineral Point.

That was when Doc announced he was going back to town too.

"They'll kill you, sure as sin," Raider said.

"Not in town, they won't," Doc said. "Only if they catch me on the way in."

Raider mounted an all-night guard at the mine, splitting the watches with Burt and Jerry. He knew they could expect more trouble, but probably not till tomorrow.

As soon as Doc hit town he went hunting for Arcady. He didn't have far to look. Right in the hotel saloon.

Arcady went deathly pale when Doc sat at his table without a word. He looked over his shoulder.

"Raider isn't here, Arcady. He's out at the Martin mine. You know Casey went out to kill them after you got rid of us for him?"

"Kill them?" Arcady looked genuinely surprised.

"If he had succeeded, you would be his accomplice," Doc said, choosing his words carefully. "I'd see to it you were brought to justice too. Not that I think the locals here would bother waiting for a judge in your case. They'd string you up in the street."

"I didn't think—"

"Yeah, I know, Arcady," Doc interrupted. "You think only about balloons and your next drink. If you go running any more errands for Mr. Thornton, you'd better start thinking about that rope round your neck. Raider and I won't be saving you. We'll be making sure the knot is tight."

As Imelda sang, Doc took sidelong looks at Cal Thornton, who had finally come out of hiding. He sat alone at a table with a bottle of Jack Daniels, but Doc could see gunslingers sprinkled about the place who looked like his hired men. Thornton would be taking no chances. Doc reckoned he was showing up at the hotel saloon deliberately to squelch those rumors he was chicken of the two Pinkertons. Doc noticed how Thornton was getting the cold shoulder from most of the miners there. He had lost their respect.

Imelda finished to loud applause and came down from the dais. Doc waited expectantly for her at the table, amused to notice that Arcady still had the hots for her, judging by the lapdog look on his face and the scornful expression on Laura's. To Doc's surprise, Imelda swept past their table without as much as a glance at him. She approached Cal Thornton. He smiled, half stood, and gestured to an empty chair. Imelda sat. Doc looked away, annoyed. It wasn't often a woman did this to him, and he was kind of unused to handling the situation.

Next time Doc glanced over, perhaps because of the sudden hush in the saloon, he saw Imelda holding a gun to Thornton's head.

Doc crossed the saloon real fast. The gun in her hand was a Colt's Third Model .41 derringer, nickel-plated and pearl-handled, elegant and deadly. Beads of perspiration ran down Cal Thornton's brow.

"All right, men," he was saying in a loud half-whisper. "Like the lady says, don't try any shooting. If you hit her, it'll be as good as flicking the hammer on this derringer."

"You rotten swine," Imelda was saying in a strange hysterical voice. "You killed the baron. Now I'm going to kill you."

"Mind if I join you?" Doc asked politely.

Thornton looked at him as if Doc were crazy. Imelda seemed unaware of Doc's arrival.

"You killed him," she was almost chanting at Thornton, seemingly about to fire. "So now you deserve to die."

"Pretty little gun, Imelda," Doc said, reaching his hand out for it. "That's the one you reloaded by turning the barrel sideways, isn't it?" Doc took it from her unresisting hand.

Pandemonium broke out. Doc spotted several of Thornton's hirelings with their Colt .45s directed at Imelda's back. He put the derringer to Thornton's forehead. The place quieted again.

Doc said, "I know Mr. Thornton doesn't want anyone here to get involved with this misunderstanding, either now or later." He looked around slowly and threateningly at the hired guns, nudging the barrel of the little gun into Thornton's forehead.

"Forget it, boys," Thornton said. "Like Doc says, it's a misunderstanding. Besides, it involves a lady." Doc withdrew the gun from his forehead and Thornton, with a look of relief, jumped to his feet. "Everybody, let's go to the Silver Spur. Drinks are on me."

Ninety percent of the customers of the hotel saloon, to the manager's horror, followed him out of the door, their previous anger at him now forgotten.

"Popular guy," Doc said and patted Imelda's hand.

She turned on him in fury. "Damn you for interfering, Doc. If it weren't for you, he would be dead now instead of treating his cronies to booze." She leaped up, grabbed her derringer, and hurried from the table.

"She'll think different tomorrow morning," Doc said, "when she wakes up in her canopy bed instead of behind bars."

Doc made for his hotel room. It had been a long day—and being an aeronaut for part of it hadn't helped. Plus the storm clouds were already piled high for tomorrow. He could use some shut-eye.

As he crossed the lobby toward the staircase, he glanced at a woman sitting in an armchair.

"Tina! What are you doing here? Is everything all right at the mine?"

"Yes."

"Oh."

"I decided to follow you into town," she said. "I asked around for you, and the porter here said that wherever that soprano was you were sure to be also. I felt a bit foolish about that, so I waited here." She smiled brightly. "I saw her go up to her room alone twenty minutes ago."

Doc looked mildly shocked. "You mean you thought the porter was suggesting that something of an intimate nature might be occurring between me and Madame Avellana?"

"Well...I'm sorry, I suppose..." Tina was embarrassed.

"Certainly we both love fine music," Doc explained. "And that I suppose forms a platonic bond between us."

"I'm sorry, Doc. I should never have made such vulgar accusations against you." She looked terribly contrite.

She let him guide her from the armchair, up the staircase, listening to his words, propelled gently forward by his discreet touch on her waist. She hardly realized he was taking off her clothes in the room, she was so lulled by his talk and the tender stroking of his hands over her smooth skin.

But as soon as he laid her naked on the bed, pulling off his own clothes and joining her, she began to change—into a fierce young animal that wants to smother death and loss with the fire and oblivion of passion. She wanted no foreplay or cuddling or kissing—she wanted him inside her, fast.

Doc grabbed her hips and pulled her toward him, while she ran the head of his cock back and forth over her clit. As raw sensation shook her body, she swore and bit him in the shoulder. When she could stand it no more, he eased her pain by driving his ramrod home, deep into her yielding sex, pumping, hammering for all he was worth, while she bucked under him like an unbroken bronco that's been eating locoweed.

She raked her fingernails down his back, twisted and turned beneath him, crying and gasping, unaware of anything but her own burning desires and fierce wants.

Doc rutted her hard and fast and pumped her so powerfully with his plunging cock that she cried for mercy— and found none. Except in the shuddering releases which came to her in wild uncontrollable orgasms. And when she thought she could bear no more and pleaded with Doc to let her rest, he cunningly started her all over again. She was his vixen, his slave of the flesh; his cock, her lord and master.

CHAPTER TWELVE

"More money?" Major Wheeler asked, as if he had never before heard such an unreasonable request in all his life.

Ouray smiled tolerantly at him over the major's desk. "You'll be a very important man in Washington when they hear how you have quieted things in the San Juan."

"Yes, yes, that matter has been concluded satisfactorily," Wheeler conceded. "Of course there's still Tahkoonica-vats—his destruction of bridges and trails is intolerable."

"Pay him no attention and he will do things from time to time. Little things. But if anyone tries to stop him, Tahkoonicavats will grow proud and begin to talk of war."

"No, no, we certainly don't want that," the major said hurriedly. "So you suggest overlooking his little peccadilloes, such as blowing up bridges and the like. I see."

"I want more money," Ouray said. "Much more money. Four times what you have been giving me."

The major was dismayed at the Ute chief's attitude. It was clear that Ouray was going to be firm in his demands. Not alone that, he seemed determined to collect the money at this very moment. Wheeler glanced at his watch. It was a little after two A.M.

Doc Weatherbee was semi-comatose from exhaustion, and his brain refused to leave the peaceful realm of sleep. But Tina was insistent.

"Sweetheart, I can't anymore," Doc moaned. "I'm wrecked. Let me get some sleep."

"It's not that, Doc," she whispered urgently. "There's someone at the door trying to get in."

Doc was awake instantly, his survival instincts honed by training and frequent use. He held his hand to her lips for silence, then slipped out of bed. Fortunately he had his Diamondback .38 in the room. He eased back the hammer. A gentle rap sounded on the door.

A voice from the other side of the door panel called softly, "It's Raider."

Doc was irritated. "What are you doing? Delivering coffee and a newspaper?"

Raider's voice was long-suffering and patient. "Tina has disappeared. We've got to search for her."

"She's with me here. Is that what you came all this way into town for?"

"Her father insisted after he missed her," Raider grumbled. "Thoughtless bitch."

"Sorry, Raider," Tina called from the bed.

"I'm going to sleep in my room down the corridor," Raider said through the door panel, for Doc had never opened the door. "Jerry and Burt can look after themselves till first light."

"Goodnight, Raider," Tina called.

She didn't catch his reply. She asked Doc, "What did he say?"

He laughed as he came back to the bed. "You're better off not knowing. It's only half true."

This got her curiosity aroused, but Doc fell asleep while she was asking him what Raider had called her.

Cal Thornton sipped from a bottle of Jack Daniels at a table in the Silver Spur, long cleared of its customers. Casey and three hired guns shared a bottle of bourbon at the next table. The only other person in the huge saloon was the fourth hired gun, passed out face down on a poker table.

"What you see here is every loose gun in town," Casey told Thornton. "I told you before, and I'm telling you now, I need a full day to round up men from nearby towns."

"I don't want to take the time," Thornton told him. "We been using brawn and numbers up till now, and where has that got us? It's time we used our brains instead of rounding up another half-assed army for them to slaughter."

Casey said nothing.

Thornton sucked moodily on the bottle of Tennessee sour mash. "Can we do anything at the mine?"

"Not with them Gatlings agin us," Casey said. "Those two brothers was practicing with them today, and I heard that the girl tried too."

"The mine is being watched round the clock?"

"Daylight hours only. Some kids are doing it for us."

"They expect us to attack there," Thornton said. "Or to try to harm Harrison. I want to go after them when and where they don't expect it."

They talked on for a while, reaching no definite conclusions. Casey was in favor of hiring a large number of men but had no particular plan of action in mind.

A knuckle rapped on a glass pane. Casey went to the door. "I thought I told you not to come here," he said to a kid in the street.

"It's important."

"It had better be," Casey said threateningly as he let him in.

Thornton looked up with interest. He threw a five-dollar gold piece on the table in front of him. "That important?"

"Yes, sir," the kid said and scooped up the coin. "I shine boots at the hotel and I tell things to Mr. Casey here. I saw Tina Martin go with Doc Weatherbee to his room. She's spending the night there."

"Run along, son," Thornton said quickly. "Say nothing to anyone."

"That's not all, sir." The boy waited expectantly.

Thornton threw another five-dollar piece on the table.

"Mr. Raider, the Pinkerton, showed up too. I heard them talking together upstairs but couldn't make out what they were saying."

Thornton beamed. "Anything else?"

"No sir."

"Go home and keep quiet."

"Yes, sir."

Casey let the kid out on the street and came back. "All three of them in town tonight . . . They got to have something big planned for tomorrow morning. And we're supposed to think they're split—Weatherbee here, Raider at the mine. We better be on our toes, boss."

"You never said a truer word, Casey. Remember what I just said about hitting them when they least expect it? Take those three men and do it now."

Casey swallowed nervously. The three hired guns climbed to their feet. This was just another job to them. They didn't know anything, having just arrived in town, broke. Casey didn't have much choice.

"I'll wait for you here," Thornton said and toasted them with his raised bottle.

Casey whacked the night porter alongside the head with his revolver before the man got a look at his face. He removed the master key from his belt, crossed the hotel lobby, and climbed the staircase, gun in hand and followed by the three hired men. His spy had described Doc's room.

On the corridor upstairs, he whispered, "There's a light on in the room. I got no way of knowing whether Raider's still there or gone back to his own room." He indicated the door of Room 23 to one of the men. "You watch for him here. You two, come with me, and let's get rid of Doc and the girl first."

He beckoned to the two men, and they made their way along the corridor to the corner room at the front of the hotel. Casey gestured to the crack of light beneath the door. The two men nodded with their gun barrels that they understood and were ready. He inserted the master key gently in the lock and turned it. It made a slight scraping noise, not enough to wake someone. Casey waited and listened intently. Then he turned the handle and pushed the door in.

Imelda Avellana sat up in bed with her Colt's Third Model .41 derringer in her right hand. The gun spat flame, and the noise of the shot resounded in the room. Casey's gun clattered to the floor. Then his knees gave way and he keeled over on the floor.

The two hired guns thought twice before shooting a beautiful woman in her bed, saw they had lost their foreman, and decided this was a job they wanted no further part of. They ran down the corridor, joined by the third.

"I heard the marshal's got a warrant for your arrest for shooting up the Silver Spur in the middle of the night, Raider," a miner said as they left town at dawn next day.

"That old hen of a marshal ain't going to bother me," Raider said. "I been wanting to do something like that a long time. After his gunmen mistook Doc's room last night, I couldn't resist it no more." He laughed at the memory. "You shoulda heard all those glasses and chandeliers and mirrors just rattling and shaking and splintering all over the place. Only thing was I had no idea Thornton himself was there till he jumped out a back window and took off into the dark. I was kinda sore I missed out on hitting him. But I hope it's what they call—what do you call that, Doc, when I hope to get it today instead?"

"A pleasure deferred."

"Right. Well, we got to be riding along. Give the marshal my regards."

Tina, Raider, and Doc rode only a little way before they ran into more miners who had also heard all about the goings-on of the previous night.

"Word travels fast," Doc said.

"We're going in tonight to hear that opera lady sing," one miner said. "Is she some kind of Calamity Jane?"

"You're in for a real surprise," Raider told him with a straight face. "I can still hardly believe her act."

Farther along the trail, they met Ouray on horseback. He seemed very happy. They learned he was on his way to see Harrison. Yes, he knew where Thornton was. He had tried to take a shortcut across Ute country to the town of Green Falls and was now lost.

"I didn't see him myself," Ouray said. "He told one of my sons he needed to hire men and that if any Ute warriors would work for him, he would give them much whiskey and guns. My sons gave him wrong directions to Green Falls. He should still be out there, lost along Cow Creek somewhere."

"Will you take us to him?" Doc asked.

The Ute chief smiled maliciously. It was plain to Doc and Raider that Ouray wished no good to Cal Thornton. However, they didn't understand things from Ouray's viewpoint, which was that Thornton as a developer of balloons was a possible future embarrassment to the Ute chief and had to be gotten rid of.

They rode with Ouray into Ute country. When they came to Cow Creek, they split into three—Doc together with Tina, and Ouray and Raider solo. They searched along both banks of the winding creek until Ouray signaled them to stop where they were. Doc and Tina were at a long stretch of rapids downriver, where the river was shallow enough to ford easily. Raider was farther upstream from them, near the opening of a defile the river cut through a ridge. Ouray rode away from the river up the ridge, the loose stones rattling downhill as his horse went back and forth across a short distance, loosening earth, pebbles, stones, and small boulders. When the earth beneath him started to slide, Ouray spurred his horse uphill till it reached solid ground again.

The slide started small but gathered boulders and rocks of increasing size on its journey down the slope. Soon it was a thundering tide of gravel, earth, and lumps of rock more than a foot across—crashing down into the defile.

A horseman galloped out of the descending shower. He was coming straight for Raider, escaping from the hail of stones, when a big boulder thumped onto the earth near his horse and nearly crushed it in a ten-foot-high bounce. The horse shied, threw the rider, and bolted.

By the time Raider rode up and dismounted, Thornton was on his feet. Pinkerton-trained to aid any man who was down, Raider was taken by surprise by the sudden menace of this cowardly and possibly wounded man.

Thornton's blue eyes blazed with hostility. "Give me your horse. Name your price, Raider. Or go for your gun."

Raider released the reins of the horse and stood feet apart in front of Thornton, hands hanging easy at his sides.

"Only place you'll be riding, Thornton, is on the end of a rope."

"You don't make peanuts, Pinkerton. Sell me your horse. I'll make you a rich man."

"Nothing doing," Raider said calmly.

"I'm getting out of here!" Thornton sounded panicky, desperate. "Sell the horse to me for gold—or I'll take him from you for nothing."

Raider laughed mockingly.

Thornton drew on him. This kind of surprised Raider, who figured him for a coward, no matter how desperate he got. Raider got another surprise in how fast Thornton could slap leather—he was almost as fast as Raider himself. Thornton even nearly managed to squeeze the trigger of his Colt .45 before Raider's .44 bullet struck him between his blue eyes and split his head apart.

Doc read the telegram from Chicago in the street outside the hotel. He, Raider, Tina, and Ouray had brought Thornton's body to the marshal's office. The marshal complained how all these bodies were costing the town a fortune to bury. He never mentioned anything about arresting Raider.

Arcady T. Harrison was visibly relieved when he saw Thornton's lifeless corpse. They could see him now through the window of the hotel saloon, celebrating at a table with Laura.

Doc read the neat copperplate hand of the Western Union clerk on the sweat-stained telegram a horseman had brought to town.

Market price for silver stocks has declined. Wall Street clients wish to write off Harrison as a loss.   Wagner

"Goddamn!" Raider said and stalked off.

Doc laughed. "I think Raider hates to find himself in agreement with New York financiers."

Ouray looked in the window of the saloon, where he was not allowed by law. The little inventor looked out and raised his glass to him. Laura smiled.

"I will keep Arcady busy," the Ute chief said and flashed a wad of bills. "I have a great belief in his talent and ability."

Doc wasn't listening. He and Tina moved hand in hand in the direction of his canopy bed.

J. D. HARDIN

"THE MOST EXCITING WESTERN WRITER SINCE LOUIS L'AMOUR"
—JAKE LOGAN

____	872-16840-9	BLOOD, SWEAT AND GOLD	$1.95
____	872-16842-5	BLOODY SANDS	$1.95
____	872-16882-4	BULLETS, BUZZARDS, BOXES OF PINE	$1.95
____	872-16877-8	COLDHEARTED LADY	$1.95
____	867-21101-6	DEATH FLOTILLA	$1.95
____	872-16844-1	THE GOOD THE BAD AND THE DEADLY	$1.95
____	867-21002-8	GUNFIRE AT SPANISH ROCK	$1.95
____	872-16799-2	HARD CHAINS, SOFT WOMEN	$1.95
____	872-16881-6	THE MAN WHO BIT SNAKES	$1.95
____	872-16861-1	RAIDER'S GOLD	$1.95
____	872-16767-4	RAIDER'S REVENGE	$1.95
____	872-16839-5	SILVER TOMBSTONES	$1.95
____	867-21133-4	SNAKE RIVER RESCUE	$1.95
____	867-21039-7	SONS AND SINNERS	$1.95
____	872-16869-7	THE SPIRIT AND THE FLESH	$1.95
____	867-21226-8	BOBBIES, BAUBLES AND BLOOD	$2.25
____	06572-3	DEATH LODE	$2.25
____	06138-8	HELLFIRE HIDEAWAY	$2.25
____	867-21178-4	THE LONE STAR MASSACRE	$2.25
____	06380-1	THE FIREBRANDS	$2.25
____	06410-7	DOWNRIVER TO HELL	$2.25
____	06152-3	APACHE GOLD	$2.25
____	06001-2	BIBLES, BULLETS AND BRIDES	$2.25
____	06331-3	BLOODY TIME IN BLACKWATER	$2.25
____	06248-1	HANGMAN'S NOOSE	$2.25
____	06337-2	THE MAN WITH NO FACE	$2.25
____	06151-5	SASKATCHEWAN RISING	$2.25
____	06412-3	BOUNTY HUNTER	$2.50
____	06743-2	QUEENS OVER DEUCES	$2.50
____	06842-0	CARNIVAL OF DEATH	$2.50
____	07017-4	LEAD LINED COFFINS	$2.50
____	06845-5	SATAN'S BARGAIN	$2.50
____	06850-1	THE WYOMING SPECIAL	$2.50
____	07259-2	THE PECOS DOLLARS	$2.50
____	07257-6	SAN JUAN SHOOTOUT	$2.50

Prices may be slightly higher in Canada.

ⓑ BERKLEY *Available at your local bookstore or return this form to:*
Book Mailing Service
P.O. Box 690, Rockville Centre, NY 11571

Please send me the titles checked above. I enclose _____. Include 75¢ for postage and handling if one book is ordered; 25¢ per book for two or more not to exceed $1.75. California, Illinois, New York and Tennessee residents please add sales tax.

NAME _____

ADDRESS _____

CITY _____ STATE/ZIP _____

(allow six weeks for delivery.)

JAKE LOGAN

___	0-872-16823	**SLOCUM'S CODE**	$1.95
___	0-867-21071	**SLOCUM'S DEBT**	$1.95
___	0-872-16867	**SLOCUM'S FIRE**	$1.95
___	0-872-16856	**SLOCUM'S FLAG**	$1.95
___	0-867-21015	**SLOCUM'S GAMBLE**	$1.95
___	0-867-21090	**SLOCUM'S GOLD**	$1.95
___	0-872-16841	**SLOCUM'S GRAVE**	$1.95
___	0-867-21023	**SLOCUM'S HELL**	$1.95
___	0-872-16764	**SLOCUM'S RAGE**	$1.95
___	0-867-21087	**SLOCUM'S REVENGE**	$1.95
___	0-872-16927	**SLOCUM'S RUN**	$1.95
___	0-872-16936	**SLOCUM'S SLAUGHTER**	$1.95
___	0-867-21163	**SLOCUM'S WOMAN**	$1.95
___	0-872-16864	**WHITE HELL**	$1.95
___	0-425-05998-7	**SLOCUM'S DRIVE**	$2.25
___	0-425-06139-6	**THE JACKSON HOLE TROUBLE**	$2.25
___	0-425-06330-5	**NEBRASKA BURNOUT #56**	$2.25
___	07182-0	**SLOCUM AND THE CATTLE QUEEN #57**	$2.75
___	07183-9	**SLOCUM'S WOMEN #58**	$2.50
___	06532-4	**SLOCUM'S COMMAND #59**	$2.25
___	06413-1	**SLOCUM GETS EVEN #60**	$2.50
___	06744-0	**SLOCUM AND THE LOST DUTCHMAN MINE #61**	$2.50
___	06843-9	**HIGH COUNTRY HOLD UP #62**	$2.50
___	07018-2	**BANDIT GOLD**	$2.50
___	06846-3	**GUNS OF THE SOUTH PASS**	$2.50
___	07046-8	**SLOCUM AND THE HATCHET MEN**	$2.50
___	07258-4	**DALLAS MADAM**	$2.50
___	07139-1	**SOUTH OF THE BORDER**	$2.50

Prices may be slightly higher in Canada.

Available at your local bookstore or return this form to:

 BERKLEY
Book Mailing Service
P.O. Box 690, Rockville Centre, NY 11571

Please send me the titles checked above. I enclose _____. Include 75¢ for postage and handling if one book is ordered; 25¢ per book for two or more not to exceed $1.75. California, Illinois, New York and Tennessee residents please add sales tax.

NAME_____

ADDRESS_____

CITY_____STATE/ZIP_____

(allow six weeks for delivery)   **162b**